DOG
BARK

To Charles
Good Luck and best
Wishes !
Gene Mullins

DOG
BARK

Gene Mullins

Northwest Publishing Inc.
Salt Lake City, Utah

Dog Bark

This is a work of fiction.
All characters and events portrayed in this book are fictional,
and any resemblance to real people or incidents is purely coincidental.

For information address: Northwest Publishing, Inc.
6906 South 300 West, Salt Lake City, Utah 84047

JC 04 14 94

PRINTING HISTORY
First Printing 1994

ISBN: 1-56901-340-3

NPI books are published by Northwest Publishing, Incorporated,
6906 South 300 West, Salt Lake City, Utah 84047.
The name "NPI" and the "NPI" logo are trademarks belonging to
Northwest Publishing, Incorporated.

PRINTED IN THE UNITED STATES OF AMERICA.
10 9 8 7 6 5 4 3 2 1

Dedication

To my wife, Beth, and my children,
Stuart, Kathy and Kara

In loving memory of
my son, Lance Mullins

Chapter One

11 May 1880

Morgan was about to turn the corner when he heard it. He stopped and listened for a moment before continuing his rounds. He checked another door, thinking, "They're louder than usual tonight...like they want me to hear them, know they are there." The thought made him intensely alert and excited him at the same time.

Morgan stepped off the boardwalk and slowly walked toward the Buffalo Saloon. His eyes swept the deserted street, scanning for movement or change. He detected nothing unusual. Four horses stood at the hitching rail. Morgan smiled wryly when he recognized the big black and the paint. His hand moved instinctively to the Colt on his hip, and he softly whispered, "Burl and Pete Gistinger!"

The hair on Morgan's neck began to crawl, and his skin goosebumped at the thought of them. Morgan wasn't afraid of them, or anybody else, but he wasn't a foolish man either. He'd learned long ago that men like Burl and Pete Gistinger were dangerous, and to go off half cocked when dealing with them would get you killed.

Morgan was three or four steps from the horses when Burl's voice reached him again. "I ain't gonna shut up, and I don't giv'a shit if th' son of a bitch hears me." His voice faded off, and Morgan heard three or four other voices. One of them mentioned him by name.

Morgan thought to himself, "Somethin' is wrong…out of place." He walked up to the big black horse and soothed, "Easy boy, easy." He patted the horse and added, "What's ol' Burl and Pete got up their sleeves tonight?" The horse skittered slightly to the left and softly whinnied. Morgan then whispered, "Be careful?" He chuckled, "I aim to."

Morgan had had numerous dealings with the Gistinger brothers during his two years as a lawman in Fort Worth, and it was common knowledge that there was bad blood between them. He had jailed them several times for being drunk, disorderly, and disturbing the peace. The latest arrest was just over a week ago. He moved away from the horses, thinking, "Burl said he'd kill me the next time. I wonder if tonight's the 'next time.'"

He moved quietly down the dark alley toward the rear of the saloon, musing, "I wonder who th' buckskin belongs to? Th' little sorrel is Blanchard's." Morgan tested the saloon's back door and found it to be open. He moved quietly inside and, once in, palmed his Colt and thumbed the sixth cartridge into the empty chamber, thinking, "I might need that extra one tonight. I've just got that feelin'."

He heard Burl's voice again, "What'd I tell you? He ain't gonna show."

Mac, the bartender, laughed sarcastically, "You hope."

"You go to hell," slurred Burl. He slammed his glass on the bar and continued, "Mac, you and everybody else in this chicken-shit town are afraid of Stuart Morgan." He belched loudly and added, "But me an' Pete ain't. Right, little brother?"

Morgan had reached the inner door that separated the back storeroom from the saloon area; the door was slightly ajar, and he pushed it open a bit more as Pete mumbled, "Damn right. I, uh, we, ain't afraid of—"

Mac cut him off, "Yeah, right. I reckon that's why you let him bust your heads and run you out of town last week. Right, boys?" He gestured to the four men playing poker at a table in the center of the saloon.

Morgan had been studying the four men and knew the man that answered. He was Karl Woodson, a local gambler.

Woodson smirked, "We'll see who's scared when—*if*—Morgan shows up."

"Ain't you one to talk," said Burl. "Guess you forgot th' time Morgan made you crawfish." Karl didn't answer. Burl continued, "'bout a year ago as I recollect." He giggled and added, "He called you a cheat an' a tin horn. Made you like it."

Woodson was fuming, but he wasn't going to tangle with Burl, at least not tonight. He nonchalantly replied, "Time wasn't right." He grinned, "Burl, if memory serves me right, Morgan's made you tuck your tail and run more'n once."

Burl stared hard at Woodson for a moment, spun back to the bar, and snarled, "Soon Karl, soon." He then threw his glass into the row of bottles behind the bar. After the sound of the breaking glass subsided, he added, "I've got bigger fish to fry tonight."

"Damn it to hell, Burl. Save it for Morgan," Mac said.

The men in the saloon continued to banter back and forth

about Morgan and the Gistinger brothers as Morgan monitored the room and the seven men. "I know everyone but th' one with his back to me," Morgan thought. The other two men at the poker table were known to him, and he dismissed them as no danger to him in the event of trouble. The unknown man chose that moment to turn his head toward the bar. The hair rose on Morgan's neck when he recognized him. Still, he smiled faintly and thought, "Of course...th' buckskin...I knew I'd seen him before, and I was right. Somethin' is wrong. It's a set-up. They might even know that I'm listenin' to them; it could be part of their plan."

An uneasy feeling crept through Morgan as he considered that possibility. He studied them some more and thought, "I could go get help. Trevor is on duty. Or, I could get Marshall Reynolds." He frowned at those thoughts and mused to himself, "I could let it pass; I only have one more day on th' job." He sighed quietly and reached the decision that was never really in doubt; he was going to go it alone and right now. It wasn't his style to back off from what had to be done. He pushed the door open and casually walked to the end of the bar, holding the Colt in his hand. Mac was the first to see him, and the shock that appeared on the bartender's face told Morgan something; they hadn't known he was in back listening. They were expecting him to come in through the bat wings.

The saloon suddenly grew silent as the others saw who Mac was staring at. Morgan noted that only the rider of the buckskin wasn't looking at him; that man showed no outward signs that he was aware of Morgan's presence, but Morgan wasn't fooled. His smile thinned as he recalled their last meeting in '77 at Fort Smith. The gunman's quickness had made a lasting impression on Morgan.

Mac broke the uneasy silence. "We were just talkin' 'bout you."

"Yeah, I heard." Morgan's voice was casual and calm. He paused for several moments, staring first at Burl and Pete, then at the men at the poker table. He continued in the same voice. "Everybody listen carefully. I'm only gonna say this one time."

Burl interrupted, "Morgan, you ain't got no—"

"Shut your mouth, Burl." The tone of Morgan's voice stopped Burl in mid-sentence. Morgan had not taken his eyes from the man with his back to him at the poker table. The saloon was once again deathly quiet. Morgan let them squirm for several seconds before he spoke again. "Charlie, Jiggs, get outta here."

The two men got up from the table and nervously moved toward the door; both stopped half-way there, and one whined, "Morgan, I had no part in this. I—"

Morgan nodded his head toward the door, "I said 'git.'" Both men bolted out the door. The bat wings were still swinging as Morgan ordered, "Karl, put your gun on the table. The gambler stared at Morgan for several seconds. Morgan stared back, and added, "Left hand, Karl…two fingers." Finally, the gambler reached under his coat and took his pistol from a shoulder holster; he slowly placed the .41 caliber pistol on the table. "Now the Derringer," ordered Morgan. Karl was mad; hatred for Morgan was evident in his eyes, but he retrieved the Derringer from his waistband and placed it on the table.

"Morgan, one of these days someone is gonna kill you."

"I expect you're right," sighed Morgan. "But who's gonna be th' first to try it?"

Morgan let this challenge sink in before he spoke again. "Mac, join Karl over at the table by the door." He nodded his head toward the table. Both men took their time moving to the table. Burl, Pete, and the stranger were motionless and quiet. Morgan was calm. After the two men sat down at the table,

Morgan ordered, "Put your hands on the table." Both men were seething inside, but they slowly put their hands on the table. "Palms down, and don't move 'em again," warned Morgan. They grudgingly obeyed.

Morgan turned to Burl and Pete, "Shuck 'em." His voice had changed from calm to stern. He moved two steps toward them and added, "I told you not to come back to town 'til I sent for you."

Pete's hands were shaking noticeably as he unbuckled his gun belt. Burl didn't move; he stood glaring at Morgan. His right hand was positioned next to the gun that he carried on his right hip; he was nervously twitching his fingers as though about to draw. "Draw it, or drop it!" snapped Morgan. He still had one eye on the man at the poker table.

Burl fumed, "Damn you Morgan…" He clawed at the buckle on his gun belt, finally got it unfastened, slung it savagely to the floor, and added, "Th' next time…" His face had turned purple, and he was having trouble speaking. Finally he managed to continue, "I'll kill you…you son of a bitch."

Morgan had by now moved down the bar and was only two feet from the brothers but was watching the stranger in the mirror behind the bar. Morgan kicked the two gun belts away and replied, "That's what you said last week. Burl, it's always next week with you. Why is that?" The two men stared into each other's eyes for several moments. Morgan smiled, "You two cowards ain't gonna kill anybody unless their back is turned." He lowered his voice and pointed to the floor, "hands and knees." Burl and Pete looked at each other and then at Morgan. The smile had disappeared entirely from Morgan's face. "Now!" he ordered.

Both men got on their hands and knees. Pete was quiet but sullen. Burl was cursing under his breath. Morgan moved to Burl and kicked him as hard as he could in the butt. The loud thump resounded in the quiet saloon.

"God damn you, Morgan!" shrieked Burl. "I'm gonna—"

Morgan kicked him again, "Burl, don't ever call my mother a bitch." He kicked him again and added, "You understand?" Morgan didn't wait for his answer. "Now crawl over to your friends." He watched the stranger, who hadn't moved or spoken. When Burl and Pete had crawled over to where Mac and Karl were seated, Morgan said, "Face down and put your hands behind your heads." Both complied. Pete was shaking. Burl was cursing.

There was silence in the room for over a minute. Morgan checked his pocket watch and quietly said, "Hmm. Nearly twelve-thirty." No one answered and Morgan continued, "You know a man can learn a lot from lookin' at a horse." He paused and added, "Now you take that buckskin outside…" Morgan's voice trailed off, and his face went dead. "I'd wager he comes from Fort Smith." Morgan was looking at Mac and Karl, and the expressions on their faces caused him to chuckle.

"I told you it wouldn't work," whined Pete. "I knew, but you—"

"Shut up!" snapped Burl.

Morgan paid them no heed; he was watching the man at the poker table. The man moved for the first time. He pushed his hat back on his head and laughed lightly, "Figured you'd remember. It was worth a try, though."

"Frank, what brings you to Fort Worth?" Morgan asked softly.

Frank Devlin moved away from the table and faced Morgan. He grinned, "I didn't think you'd remember me." His grin widened, and he added, "Guess I was wrong. My mistake."

Morgan holstered his pistol and quietly replied, "I never forget a rattlesnake, Frank." Morgan moved a step away from the bar and continued. "Your mistake was comin' out from under th' rock you've been hidin' under since '77." Morgan saw his words had hit home. The gunman's eyes turned to hard slits, and his face paled then reddened. Morgan thought, "That's it. Get mad. Get good and mad."

Frank regained his composure some and laughed, "Same old Morgan. Always got somethin' clever to say." He took one step to his left and added, "I ain't forgot '77." He took another step to his left. "A man don't forget his best friend's murder."

Morgan knew that Frank was moving to get between him and the other men and to center him. He moved one step to his right and said, "Tony Slater got what he asked for."

"He had no chance against you, Morgan, and you know it." Frank's voice was noticeably higher. He was clenching and unclenching his right hand.

"He had the same chance as you've got tonight."

"Meaning?"

"He could've walked away and lived." Morgan smiled slightly and added, "Frank, death comes soon enough. Only fools go lookin' for it."

Frank licked his lips. "I'm faster'n Slater."

"Yeah, I know," deadpanned Morgan. "But I'm still gonna get one in you." He was thinking, "He's gonna do th' same thing he did that time at Fort Smith when he killed that drunk. He's gonna turn away, turn back, gesture with his left hand and draw." Morgan visualized what he had seen that day at Fort Smith and thought, "Human nature is predictable. He'll try it again."

The gunman stood frozen, thinking, staring at Morgan. He finally whispered, "Some other time, Morgan." He slowly turned away, took two steps, and turned back toward Morgan.

As soon as Frank moved his left arm, Morgan quickly turned a half step to his right and drew; the Colt belched flame and smoke at the same instant Frank's slug tugged at his left shirt sleeve and shattered the bar mirror behind him. Morgan's aim was straight and true; his bullet struck Devlin in the heart with such force that the gunman was sent crashing backwards into a ceiling support post. Although Devlin was dead on his feet, he momentarily stood there, gazing at Morgan with disbelief in his eyes. Morgan watched with cool detachment as the gunman pitched forward onto his face, his gun thudding loudly to the floor in the silent saloon.

Morgan saw movement from the direction of the table where the four men were. His Colt spoke again. The well-aimed shot splintered the back of a chair not six inches from Woodson's right shoulder. "I told you not to move," warned Morgan.

Morgan pointed the gun back to the prone gunman and carefully moved toward him. Just as he leaned over him a voice called out. "Morgan, it's me, Marshall Reynolds. We're comin' in."

"Come on in," answered Morgan. Reynolds came in the front bat wings carrying a double-barreled shotgun. Deputy Trevor Carrigan came in from the back; he had a rifle. Both lawmen surveyed the room before joining Morgan.

"Who've we got here?" asked Reynolds.

Morgan turned Devlin over on his back with the toe of his boot. "Name's Frank Devlin. Gunman, hired killer."

Trevor whistled softly, "From Fort Smith?"

"One and th' same," answered Morgan.

By now several men, including Jiggs Blanchard, began to filter into the saloon. Reynolds turned toward them, "Everybody out!" They all started to move out of the building. Reynolds spoke again, "Jiggs, stay."

The little man smiled nervously, "I saw it all, Marshall." He pointed to the front window, looked apprehensively at Burl and Pete, who by now were on their feet, and continued, "Devlin pulled on Morgan. Saw it all through that thar winder."

Morgan had by now moved over to the bar and was leaning

casually against it; he was staring stoically at Burl, Pete, Karl, and Mac as he ejected the two shell casings from his pistol. Morgan deftly punched a cartridge into one of the empty chambers, spun the cylinder, placed the hammer on the empty chamber, and holstered the gun.

Reynolds went over to the men. "You heard what Jiggs said." He paused for several moments, stared with icy eyes at them and asked, "Is he tellin' it right?"

"Devlin didn't…" Mac stopped in mid-sentence when he saw the looks Burl and Karl gave him.

"Devlin didn't do what?" asked Reynolds.

Mac laughed nervously, "Nothin', Marshall. I didn't see nothin'." He glanced at Burl and added, "It all happened so fast."

Reynolds stared at Mac then turned to Karl, "What'd you see, gamblin' man?"

Karl didn't bat an eye. "Same as Mac. I didn't see nothin'."

"Nothin,' huh?" chortled Reynolds. "Man's shot right in front of you." He shrugged his shoulders, "And you two birds didn't see nothin'." He turned to Burl and Pete. "What about it?"

Pete blurted out, "I wuz—"

Burl interrupted, "We didn't see nothin' either." He shot a hard look at Morgan and added sarcastically, "Th' big man had us layin' face down." Burl looked at Pete and continued, "Ain't that right, Pete?"

Pete was staring at the floor. "Face down we wuz, with our hands behind our heads." He looked timidly at Morgan and whined, "Ain't that right, Deputy Morgan?"

Morgan didn't reply. Reynolds walked to the bar and stood next to Morgan. "Stuart, you heard 'em," he mocked. "They didn't see nothin'."

"They're all lyin' through their teeth," said Morgan. His voice was void of emotion, and his face had gone dead as well.

Reynolds sighed, "Figured as much."

Trevor chimed in, "A swift kick in the butt sometimes cures bad eyesight."

"Nolan, it was a set-up. They're all in it up to their eyeballs," said Morgan. He sauntered over to the four men, stared hard at them for several moments, and whispered, "And that's the truth of it, ain't it boys?"

"You can't prove jack shit, Morgan," spat Burl. "And you know it."

Woodson smiled wryly, "Now that Devlin's cashed in—"

Morgan was quiet for a while, then he turned to Mac. "I know you got somethin' to say, Mac."

Before Mac could reply, Trevor interrupted, "He should. He's got th' biggest mouth in town."

Mac shot Trevor a mean look. "Like I said, I didn't see nothin' and I don't know nothin' about no set-up." He cleared his throat and added, "And I'll swear to it in a court of law."

Morgan looked at Pete. Pete looked away. "I see," sighed Morgan. "So that's the way it's gonna be." He turned to walk away, then suddenly whirled and delivered a wicked blow to the unsuspecting Burl's midsection. The blow knocked the air out of the big man and drove him to his knees. Morgan turned to Reynolds and Carrigan. "I didn't see nothin'."

Both lawmen shook their heads, "I didn't see nothin'."

Burl staggered to his feet and wheezed, "You bastards have your fun while you can, cause I ain't forgettin' this."

"Is that a threat?" asked Trevor, his voice flat.

Burl shot back, "It's any damn thing you want it to be."

"I've heard enough of your bull, Burl," snapped Reynolds. "Now shut your yap...all of you!" He turned to Morgan, "Morgan, it's your choice. We can jail 'em if you want."

Morgan thought for a moment. "Let 'em go." The room grew very quiet. Burl broke the silence.

"This ain't the end."

"Burl, you're finally right about somethin'. It isn't th' end." Morgan's eyes were now pitch black and hard. He stared at Burl for several moments and continued, "Th' end is when you're six feet under."

Burl shot back, "I'll be around long enough to piss on your grave."

"Talk's cheap," answered Reynolds. "Now get movin'." Burl and Pete started for their guns but were stopped by Morgan.

"Leave 'em!"

Both men whirled and stomped toward the bat wings. Burl pushed the wings open and stopped. "Morgan, I hear this is your last day on the job…you're headin' west."

"You heard right."

Burl chuckled, "Lot of things can happen to a man out on th' trail by his lonesome."

"I suppose," Morgan casually answered.

"Like I said, I ain't gonna forget you kickin' me, hittin' me when I wasn't lookin'." He then looked at Jiggs. "I ain't forgettin' you either, Jiggs."

Jiggs stammered, "Now Burl, you got no—"

Morgan interrupted, "Burl, if I run into you on th' trail, there's not gonna be any talkin', leastways not on my part." The two men were quiet for several seconds, their eyes locked. Burl was the first to look away; he finally stomped out. Morgan called after him. "Same goes for Pete. Tell him!"

Woodson spoke up. "Can I go?"

"Yep," answered Reynolds. "All th' way outta Fort Worth."

Woodson replied in a shaky voice, "Marshall, you runnin' me outta town?"

"For your own good," smiled Reynolds. "Fort Worth is too dangerous a place for a man who can't see." He winked at Morgan and Carrigan, "'Sides, a blind gambler'd be easy pickin's for our local riff raff and such."

Woodson was raging inside. He got up, thinking, "I'm

gonna fix these bastards. Ain't nobody ever got away…" He moved toward the table to his guns.

Reynolds stopped him in his tracks. "Leave 'em lay." Woodson spun around and glowered at Reynolds; he was visibly shaking. Reynolds was smiling. "When you get to where you're goin', get word to me. I'll send 'em to you."

Woodson stared at the guns for a moment and then turned and walked away. After he had gone, Trevor said, "We'd better watch our backs for a spell."

"That's a fact," replied Reynolds. He turned to Jiggs. "Jiggs, go fetch th' undertaker. Tell him he's got a customer."

"I'm on my way." Jiggs stopped at the door and said, "Marshall, Burl's gonna—"

"You leave Burl to us." The Marshall's voice was calm and reassuring.

Morgan said, "Jiggs, we'll need your statement."

Jiggs was thinking, "I wish I'd kept my mouth shut," but he stammered, "Sure thing, Morgan." He licked his lips and added, "First thing tomorrow mornin'."

After Jiggs had gone, Reynolds said, "We ain't forgot about you, Mac."

Mac had moved behind the bar and was casually wiping the bar with a rag. "Marshall, you got no call to run me outta town."

"Who said anything about runnin' you out of town?"

His reply caught Mac by surprise; he was speechless for a moment. Mac finally stammered, "I didn't know they were gonna—"

Morgan cut him off. "Mac, you're a liar and a coward." He stared with cold, hard eyes at the nervous bartender. After several moments of uneasy silence, Morgan said, "Nolan, the buckskin outside belongs to Devlin."

"I'll take him over to th' livery," offered Trevor.

Morgan nodded his head to Trevor and said to Reynolds,

"I'll write my report before I go off duty."

"Do it in th' mornin'," Reynolds said. "Go ahead and turn in. Me an' Trevor can handle things." Morgan started to protest, but Reynolds waved him off. "Hell, you've had a full night, Besides, I'm already up. Couldn't go back to sleep if I wanted to."

Morgan knew the old lawman well enough not to argue with him. "See you come first light," he said.

After Morgan left, Carrigan turned to Mac. "I wouldn't want to be in your shoes."

Mac glowered at the deputy. "And what's that suppose to mean?"

Reynolds answered. "Meaning Morgan knows what you rats were up to tonight."

"Like I said," mumbled Mac. "I didn't—"

"See nothin' or know nothin'," interrupted Reynolds. He smiled at Mac and added, "Morgan's got you pegged." He swung up the shotgun, pointed it at the bartender and continued, "He ain't th' type to forget a weasel like you." He lowered the gun and walked away.

Trevor had just finished gathering up Karl's and the Gistingers' guns; he smiled wryly at Mac and followed Reynolds to the door. When the lawman reached the entrance, Trevor called over his shoulder, "Morgan's headin' west tomorrow, Mac. If I was you, I'd head east."

After he was sure they'd gone, Mac cursed, "Goddamned bastards." He slammed his right fist into his left palm, thinking, "Th' hell with this damn place...I've been thinkin' of goin' to New Orleans anyway."

Morgan left the saloon feeling like he always felt after killing a man; loneliness began to seep deep into his soul. He walked down the dark, deserted street, thinking, "It's always th' same, just like th' first time. Why do I feel this way? Devlin needed killin'."

Morgan opened the door to Ferguson's boarding house and mused, "Just like th' rest of 'em." Then he thought, "Except th' Kiowa." He went to his room, lay on the bed and stared at the dark ceiling. As was the case after the other seven times he had killed, he was forced to relive each one as they appeared vividly behind his eyes in color and in slow motion.

He was watching Devlin draw his gun; he saw his and the gunman's guns spurt flame and smoke almost simultaneously. He heard the deafening roar that the two Colts made and saw dust fly from Devlin's vest as his bullet struck him. Morgan thought, "I didn't remember seein' him draw…or seein' th' flames…smoke…hearin' th' sound of guns firin'…th' dust flyin' from him—"

The scene continued to unfold behind Morgan's closed eyes. He saw the shock on Devlin's face and the look of disbelief that showed in his eyes. Morgan watched him pitch forward, and he heard the sound that Devlin's gun made as it hit the floor in the then quiet saloon. He saw the astonishment in Woodson's and Mac's faces. He faintly heard Burl say, "Kill the breed son of a bitch." He could see Jiggs' face through the front window. The little man's eyes were big and bright.

Morgan finally dozed off, only to dream over and over of Devlin, the Kiowa brave, the others, and his father, who had been shot and killed by a robber when Morgan was only thirteen years old. In his dreams that night, a strange thing happened. Devlin's face changed into the Kiowa's as Morgan saw the dust fly from his vest. The expression on the Kiowa's face was the same as it was that cold December day in '68 when Morgan was forced to shoot the Indian; it was one of joy and hatred, one not dominant over the other.

Morgan awoke from his dreams and immediately thought, "He was th' only one that shouldn't have died." He let his mind clear for a moment and said aloud in the dark room. "Yet, he was th' only one who seemed ready to die." Morgan recalled the look in the Kiowa's eyes as he died; it was a look of expectance and acceptance.

He swung his feet to the floor, thinking, "Th' others had fear, shock, and surprise in theirs." He momentarily pushed those thoughts from his mind as he poured water in the basin and washed his face and hands. He put on a clean shirt, thinking, "After breakfast I'll get a shave and a haircut. I've got a lot to do if I'm leaving tomorrow."

Morgan busied himself getting his belongings together while thinking about the night before. "It's a good time to move on." He knew that everybody in town would want to hear his version of the killing. He combed his hair, thinking, "They can hear about it from Mac or Jiggs or Burl." He looked at his reflection in the mirror and mused, "Burl oughtta have his story straight by now."

Morgan was disciplined and predictable, and this morning would not be an exception; he cleaned and checked his gun. After doing so, he practiced his draw for a full ten minutes. He did it standing, sitting, and laying down. Morgan then repeated the drills left-handed, using a left-handed holster and gun belt. He took off the left-handed rig, thinking, "I'm nearly there...almost as fast. A few more weeks should do it. Hit eight outta ten targets last week. Not bad considering I hit only two outta ten that first time." He left his room, thinking, "My last day in Fort Worth. Time to move on."

Chapter Two

Morgan checked his watch. It was still only a little after eight. He'd eaten breakfast, filled out his report concerning the shooting of Devlin, and had gotten a shave and a haircut. Morgan closed the door to the barber shop, thinking, "They'll have Devlin eight feet tall and faster'n Earp and Hardin before day's end."

As he stepped onto the street, Morgan heard the barber say, "Devlin was fast, but Morgan got five shots off before he cleared leather."

Another man said, "Cool customer, that Morgan. Just killed a man, and he's actin' like nothin' has happened."

Morgan smiled wryly and thought, "I wonder how a man's

supposed to act after he's killed a man." He was aware that all the people along the street had stopped and were staring at him. He thought, "I'm glad I'm leavin'. Damn fools think killin' a man is somethin' special." He shook his head and thought, "If they only knew. Oh, th' hell with 'em. Maybe a few days alone on the trail will cure what ails me."

Morgan entered the office to find Reynolds talking with a stranger. "Mornin', Stuart," greeted Reynolds. "I want you to meet Wallace McEachern."

Morgan walked over to the two men and stuck out his hand to McEachern. As they shook hands, Reynolds added, "Wallace is the new U.S. Marshall assigned to our region."

McEachern smiled, "Pleased to meet you, Morgan."

"Same here."

"Marshall Reynolds tells me you've done me a favor."

"Oh?"

Reynolds interrupted, "Devlin shot a man last week up in th' Nations."

"Any idea what he was doin' down here?" asked McEachern.

"I can't prove it, but I suspect he was sent for by Burl Gistinger," answered Morgan. "I don't think it took much proddin' though to get him here. I had to kill a friend of his back in '77."

McEachern nodded his head, "I don't mind tellin' you. I wasn't lookin' forward to tanglin' with him. I'm obliged to you."

"He didn't give me any options. It was him or me," sighed Morgan.

McEachern changed the subject. "Nolan tells me you're pullin' up stakes, handin' in your badge and goin' to California."

Morgan unpinned his badge and placed it on the desk. "Reckon I am." He paused and stared at the badge for a moment. "I've been here over two years." His eyes moved from the badge to Reynolds, and he continued, "Longest I've stayed anywhere since I left San Antonio in '64." Morgan's and Reynolds' eyes locked for a moment. Both smiled as a mutual understanding passed between them.

Reynolds stood up and said, "I'm gonna miss you, Stuart." There was a gathering of mist in the old lawman's eyes. They shook hands, and Reynolds asked, "You thought any more about Dog Bark?"

Morgan sighed, "I appreciate the offer Marshall, but my mind's made up. I'm gonna visit a friend at Fort Griffin for a few days and—"

"Dog Bark's only a day's ride from Griffin," interrupted Reynolds. He smiled and added, "Probably wouldn't take you more'n a week or two to clean up that mess." He winked at McEachern.

Morgan shook his head. "Thanks, but no thanks. My mind's made up."

Reynolds picked up a piece of paper from his desk and handed it to Morgan. "Suit yourself. If you change your mind, give this to the sheriff there. Name's Luther Piper."

Morgan took the letter and saw that it was a letter of introduction. He folded the letter and put it in his pocket. "He ask for help?"

"Nope. That ain't Luther's style. Just thought since you're goin' that way—"

Morgan changed the subject. "I hear that renegade Indian is still raisin' hell around Fort Griffin and Dog Bark."

McEachern answered, "And in Oklahoma, Kansas, and Colorado, if you believe all the reports." He smiled wryly and added, "Hell, ain't no way one Indian could be everywhere they claim him to have been."

Reynolds chuckled, "The army says he's Comanche— one of Quanah's boys who refused to go in."

"He's not Comanche," said Morgan. His voice was flat.

Reynolds and McEachern looked at each other and then at Morgan. "He's Kiowa," said Morgan. Before the two men could say anything, Morgan said, "Pleasure meetin' you, Marshall." He turned to Reynolds, "Thanks for everything." The two men stared at each other for a moment. Morgan finally nodded to Reynolds and then started to say something, but changed his mind and walked quickly toward the door.

Reynolds and McEachern didn't speak for a while after Morgan left; they just gazed at the door. Reynolds cleared his throat. "He remind you of anyone?"

McEachern thought for a moment, "Can't say he does."

"That's what makes him different, special," replied Reynolds. "He don't remind you of nobody. Morgan's one of a kind." He sighed and went on, "Best deputy I ever had."

McEachern was deep in thought as he listened to the marshall talk about Morgan, "He might just be the man we're looking for. Tell me about him."

Reynolds went to a roll-top desk and retrieved a folder from one of the drawers; he returned to his desk and began to read. "Stuart Lee Morgan, born 15 July 1848; San Antonio, Texas." Reynolds cleared his throat and continued, "Grand-mother on his mother's side…quarter Comanche…mother… Mexican…father owned livery…shot and killed by a man named Jubal Carver. Morgan was thirteen at th' time…" Reynolds stopped and looked at McEachern.

McEachern was thinking, "I thought he was a little dark…and that nose…eyes…" McEachern mused, "Eyes… almost pitch black. Seems to look clear through you."

"First thing you notice when you meet him." Reynolds started reading again, "Five eleven; one eighty-five." He closed the folder and said, "Well, you get th' picture."

"I'm startin' to," replied McEachern. "What else can you tell me?"

"Not much. Morgan don't talk much about his past."

Reynolds paused, shrugged his shoulders, and continued, "Matter of fact he don't say much about anything. Most of what I know was told to me by Captain Coldiron. He and Morgan are friends, served together with MacKenzie. Coldiron's either at Fort Griffin or Fort Concho. I don't recollect which."

"He th' friend Morgan mentioned goin' to visit?"

"Most likely," answered Reynolds. "As I was sayin', Morgan left San Antonio lookin' for Jubal Carver when he was sixteen. Coldiron said he followed leads all over Texas, Oklahoma, Kansas, and Colorado."

Reynolds went to the stove and poured coffee into two cups; he handed one to McEachern and continued, "Morgan scouted and hunted for th' army from '66 to '75. Got to know th' Comanche and th' Kiowa real good."

"I hear Morgan speaks three or four languages," commented McEachern.

"Comanche, Kiowa, and Mexican," answered Reynolds. "He served as interpreter at Th' Treaty at Medicine Lodge in '67." Reynolds smiled and continued about Morgan's past. "He was at Palo Duro with Colonel Mackenzie in '74..." Reynolds' voice lowered as he sighed and said, "Coldiron told me Stuart was so shocked and depressed by that Palo Duro slaughter...killing off all those Indian horses."

Reynolds didn't finish the sentence; he was again staring at the door. McEachern cleared his throat. "Morgan quit th' army right after Palo Duro didn't he?"

"Right. Right after," replied Reynolds. "Winter of '75, I believe." Reynolds poured himself another cup of coffee and nodded to McEachern. McEachern shook his head, and Reynolds continued. "Morgan was a deputy at Fort Smith and San Antonio for several years before he came to work for me in...let me think..." He scratched his head and said, "In April of '78."

Neither spoke for several moments. McEachern broke the silence. "I hear he's fast."

"Faster'n most," Reynolds replied. He looked at his hands and added, "I've seen faster. Matter of fact I was probably a shade faster than him myself...back in my prime..." His thoughts turned inward, and his eyes focused far off in space. He finally added, "Course I'd have ended up like th' others who tried him."

"How's that?" asked McEachern.

"Dead as a doornail." Reynolds said it calmly and matter-of-factly; he smiled wryly and continued, "I've never seen anybody like him...so cool and determined. Fearless, he is...once his mind is made up, he never backs off. He's relentless when he thinks he's right."

McEachern listened to Reynolds, thinking, "He's my man, all right...Jubal Carver just might be the edge I need."

Reynolds was saying, "Ben Thompson's th' only other man who might stand a chance; he'd have to be lucky though." Reynolds paused again, deep in thought. McEachern sat quietly and waited for the old lawman to resume speaking. "Morgan's smart...and clever, damn clever. Wallace, we had two unsolved murders here when he came. He solved 'em in no time flat." Mist came into his eyes again as he whispered, "He's been like a son." Reynolds again struggled with the frog in his throat and added, "Best deputy I ever had...gonna miss him somethin' awful."

13 May 1880

Morgan had packed only the bare essentials for his trip; a small coffee pot, a tin cup, a small tin plate, a fork, a spoon, a canteen, one blanket, a poncho, and his army field glasses. In the way of food-stuffs, he packed coffee, jerked beef, and some biscuits, with the thought of hunting for his fresh meat. For clothing, he brought two shirts, two additional pairs of

socks, and a light fur-lined jacket. He was armed with his Colt
.45, a Winchester repeating rifle, a spare Colt .45 pistol, a
Sharps hunting rifle, a hatchet, and his hunting knife. He also
carried four boxes of ammunition for the pistols and the
Winchester, and twenty-five rounds for the Sharps, and the
left-handed holster and gun belt. Morgan was dressed in
denims and a gray cotton shirt, black low-heeled boots, and a
black low-crowned hat.

He had been on the trail for over an hour when the Texas
sun peeked over the horizon. Morgan stopped his horse fifty
yards off the trail, watching his back trail. Morgan sat perfectly still for several moments, looking and listening. Although he hadn't heard or seen anyone, he sensed that someone or something was back there.

Morgan patted the horse on the neck. "Ebon, maybe I was
wrong." He pressed lightly with his knees, and the horse
moved off at a slow walk. Morgan whispered, "Keep your ears
open. I ain't usually wrong."

He walked the horse parallel to the worn trail that most
riders used when going from Fort Worth to Fort Griffin.
Morgan, a cautious man, rarely rode the known trails; besides,
he wasn't in any hurry to reach Fort Griffin. He was enjoying
the feeling that being alone on the frontier brought him.

Morgan turned to the left and said, "Ebon, let's double
back and see who's followin' us." Morgan crossed the trail
and rode south for several minutes, then turned east. He
walked the horse for a hundred yards or so and stopped.
Morgan was thinking, "It could be a stranger." Morgan
thought some more on it and mused, "Or it could be Burl and
Pete." Then another thought sent chills through him. "Th'
Kiowa?"

The thought of the Kiowa triggered a flood of images and
stirred feelings in Morgan, but he was jolted back to the
present when he saw movement. A horse and rider were

slowly moving adjacent to the main trail. Morgan watched them for awhile and whispered, "He's trackin' us all right, Ebon." He watched awhile, and after he was satisfied that the rider was alone, Morgan turned and backtracked to the trail.

As he tied the gray to a small mesquite tree, he pondered, "Can't make him out…he's not an Indian, and it's not Burl or Pete." Morgan rubbed Ebon's neck and soothed, "Stand easy, boy. Let's find out what's on this ol' boy's mind." Morgan checked his gun and moved behind a cottonwood tree that concealed him but still allowed him to observe the trail. Morgan didn't have to wait long before the rider came around a small stand of mesquite trees. Morgan's face creased into a frown as he recognized the rider.

Morgan stepped out of hiding just as the trailing rider passed. "If I was th' Kiowa, you'd be dead by now."

Momentarily startled by the unexpected voice, the tracker turned his horse and replied, "I expect so, but I wasn't trackin' th' Kiowa." McEachern smiled and added, "I was hoping you'd ask questions first." Slipping easily off his horse he continued, "Reynolds said you were a cautious man. You must have doubled back five times since you left this mornin'." McEachern's voice was friendly, and he had a wide smile on his face.

"Six," replied Morgan. His voice was flat.

McEachern chuckled, "I guess a man can't be too careful."

Morgan thought, "He wants somethin' mighty bad to go to all this trouble," but he said, "I learned a long time ago that careless men in a hurry out here wind up dead more often than not."

"I've heard that," replied McEachern, staring into Morgan's black eyes for a moment. He added, "I suppose you're wonder'n why I'm out here."

Morgan replied, "It crossed my mind."

"I need your help."

The two men looked at each other for a moment, each measuring the other. "I won't track th' Kiowa," stated Morgan.

McEachern laughed, "No, that's not what I had in mind. I got a tougher job for you."

"If it's a law job, I'm not interested," Morgan said.

"It's a law job all right, and it requires a special man." McEachern paused, looked Morgan right square in the eyes and added, "I believe you're that special man. Stuart, hear me out, and if you're still not interested, I'll skedaddle on back to Fort Worth. No hard feelin's. Fair enough?"

Morgan thought for a moment and said, "Fair enough." He was thinking, "No matter what it is, I ain't takin' it."

"I want you to go to Dog Bark as an undercover Deputy U.S. Marshall." McEachern paused, and when Morgan showed no sign of commenting, he added, "I've got your appointment and badge in my saddlebags." McEachern paused again and said, "The job pays one hundred a month."

A faint smile appeared on Morgan's face. "A hundred, huh."

McEachern smiled back. "Yep, one hundred, and the first month is in advance."

"Must be dangerous."

"Very." McEachern was now somber and his voice was low. "Th' first man we sent has disappeared, and two other local deputies have been killed." McEachern's eyes bored into Morgan as he asked, "Still not interested?"

Morgan had no idea why, but in that instant he knew he was going to take the job. "Maybe," he answered. "What's th' problem at Dog Bark?"

"You name it. Murder, robbery, lynchings, budding range war, rustling, beatings—all this in addition to th' regular problems of town—"

"Sounds like a job for th' rangers and th' army," interrupted Morgan.

McEachern deadpanned, "I told my boss and th' governor that you'd have it cleaned up by end of June." He chuckled as he saw the look of astonishment on Morgan's face. "They've agreed to hold off sendin' 'em."

Morgan grinned, "Of all th' low-down gall." His grin widened, and he continued, "Pretty sure of yourself weren't you."

"Sorta. I hedged my bets."

"How so?"

McEachern laughed, "After talkin' to Marshall Reynolds, I was pretty sure you'd do it. I was right, wasn't I?"

Morgan gazed into McEachern's eyes for several seconds. "I reckon you were at that."

McEachern rubbed his hands together. "Good!" I knew in my bones I could count on you." He went to his saddlebags, got an envelope, and handed it to Morgan. "Here's your letter of appointment, your badge, and one hundred dollars."

Morgan took the envelope. "Does Marshall Reynolds know?"

"No. Only my boss, myself, and you." McEachern's smile disappeared, and his voice thickened with concern as he continued. "Stuart, I'm convinced that your stayin' alive and the success of this operation depends on keepin' our secret between just the three of us." He became more solemn and added, "The governor doesn't even know your name."

Morgan took out a small notebook and pencil that he always carried. "Reynolds said the sheriff at Dog Bark was named Piper. He th' only law there?"

McEachern frowned, "Piper's the county sheriff. Pretty much runs the county. Casts a long shadow. He's a big man, six three or so…weighs about two thirty. Piper's got two deputies working for him."

Morgan looked up from his notebook. "Names?"

"Tiny Leatherwood and Jack Rideout." McEachern chuckled, "'Tiny!' I hear he's close to three hundred pounds."

Morgan wrote their names in his notebook and then asked, "You got any dirt on Piper?"

The frown returned to McEachern's face; he shrugged his shoulders and replied, "Nothing major, but we've had some complaints on him and Leatherwood."

Morgan thought for a moment. "Find out all you can about them and get back to me."

"I'll do it. Anything else I can do?"

"Yes, there is. Find out who's complaining about Piper and Leatherwood."

McEachern smiled, "Doc O'Banion and Myles Witherspoon." Morgan stared at McEachern for a moment and wrote their names. McEachern continued, "O'Banion's th' sawbones at Dog Bark. Myles Witherspoon's th' editor of th' *Dog Bark Clarion*."

Morgan wrote some more in the notebook before asking, "What's th' missing deputy's name?"

"Chris Walsh," sighed McEachern. "He was a good man...seasoned; fair hand with a gun, too...." His voice faded, and his eyes watered.

Morgan wrote again, thinking, "They must have been close." He gave McEachern time to compose himself before he asked, "Anything else I should know?"

McEachern cleared his throat, "They're on th' verge of a range war there...between Jedd Killpatrick and Jessie Haggard. Killpatrick owns th' Kiowa Lance, Haggard th' Circle H."

"Water or grass?"

"Neither," answered McEachern. "And that's what's puzzling us. Both are big spreads with plenty of water."

"Hmm," said Morgan.

McEachern continued, "Both blame th' other for their problems."

"Such as?"

"Missing stock, mostly, and both sides have had punchers bushwhacked."

Morgan wrote again in his notebook and put it in his shirt pocket, saying, "Who's Piper sidin' with?"

"Hard to say," replied McEachern. "Accordin' to our information, he ain't helpin' either one of 'em."

"Uh-huh." Morgan thought for a moment and asked, "Are there any farmers in th' county?"

"Only three or four are left; rest of 'em pulled up stakes. Several were killed, and some had their places burned down."

"Killpatrick and Haggard involved?" asked Morgan.

"Don't know for sure," answered McEachern. He raised his eyebrows and added, "Most folks down there believe that renegade Indian is responsible. Seems there were Indian signs everywhere…" McEachern spoke again after a short pause. "Kiowa, you said. What'd you say his name was?"

The mention of the Kiowa, as always, plunged Morgan deep into thought, "First saw him in 1867…Treaty at Medicine Lodge." The image of the Kiowa sent a cold shiver down his spine and made his skin goosebump. His mind carried him back to that day in the buffalo wallow when he killed the Kiowa warrior. The sound of McEachern's voice brought Morgan back to the present.

"Are you all right?"

"Now it's coming back to me," whispered Morgan. "He was there that day, too." He was staring off into space.

"Who was? What day?"

Morgan quietly said, "His name's Bear Paw." He turned to McEachern and continued, "The Kiowas that came in said he was dead…caught the pox…but don't you believe it. I don't. It's him; he's th' only one capable of doin' all of this…he's th' fiercest…bravest Indian I ever encountered.

Both men were caught up in their own thoughts, and

neither spoke for a spell. Finally McEachern said, "Stuart, I'm goin' back to Fort Worth for a day or two, and then you can reach me at Fort Griffin. I'm not known there. I'll be usin' th' name 'Will Taylor' and posin' as a cattle buyer."

Morgan nodded his head. "I'm goin' to Griffin and palaver with Coldiron before moseyin' down to Dog Bark."

McEachern, climbing back on his horse, said, "Today's the thirteenth. I'll be at Fort Griffin on the sixteenth or seventeenth." He turned his horse around and continued, "Burl and Pete have dropped out of sight. I thought you'd like to know."

A faint smile crossed Morgan's mouth. "I figured as much."

"Be careful," warned McEachern.

"You can count on it."

McEachern sat his horse and studied Morgan. "You look like a man who's still got somethin' on his mind," Morgan inquired.

McEachern leaned down to Morgan. "I suppose I do." He paused for a long while before adding, "Stuart, I was gonna tell you this even if you'd turned me down."

Morgan didn't answer. He was thinking, "I had a hunch there was more."

"One of our informants tells us that Jubal Carver may be in the Griffin, Dog Bark area."

The mention of Jubal Carver made Morgan's heart skip a beat, and a cold, sour feeling slid all the way to his stomach. His eyes turned pitch black, and he didn't speak right away. He was thinking back to the day Carver had killed his father and of all the days he'd spent searching for him. Morgan finally said, "What name's he goin' by?" His voice was flat as was his face.

"He didn't say."

Morgan nodded his head, thinking, "No matter. If he's there, I'll find him."

"If you find him, let th' law hang him." McEachern's voice was casual.

"It'll be his option," replied Morgan.

McEachern sighed, "Good luck." They shook hands, and McEachern started back down the trail. He called over his shoulder, "End of June, Stuart. End of June."

Morgan watched McEachern for a moment, then went to his horse and got his field glasses from his saddlebags. He climbed up a cottonwood tree and watched until McEachern disappeared from view, then climbed down, thinking, "I'm gettin' jumpy. Even McEachern resembles him."

Chapter Three

Morgan waited and watched his backtrail after McEachern left. Only after he was satisfied that McEachern hadn't been followed did he move. He rode a half mile farther north of the main trail, found a secluded spot, and waited there for over an hour. When he was certain that no one had followed him, he rode slowly west again, parallel to the main trail, stopping often to look and listen; he didn't hear or see anything unusual.

After riding for about an hour, drifting slowly westward toward the Brazos River and Fort Griffin, Morgan turned back to the south after crossing the trail to Abilene, Kansas. He then crossed the main trail to Fort Griffin and continued on south for five or six hundred yards, doubled back two hundred yards, and stopped. "This is a good place to camp for th' night…that hollow behind th' stand of cottonwoods and cedars will do fine. Someone would have to know you're there to see or find you," he mused to himself.

Morgan turned the gelding toward the trees and whispered, "Ebon, if memory serves me right, just a mite west of here, there should be a creek with sweet runnin' water." Ebon nickered quietly, and Morgan added, "After we make camp, we'll mosey over there and have us a cool drink."

There was still over an hour of daylight left when Morgan returned from the creek. He turned Ebon loose to graze, knowing the gelding wouldn't stray very far. He placed his freshly-filled canteen down beside his saddle and blanket, thinking, "I owe Coldiron one. Ebon's one fine piece of horseflesh." Coldiron had found the gray out on the staked plains the summer after the battle at Palo Duro and had given him to Morgan shortly thereafter.

Morgan whistled softly and Ebon came to him immediately. He scratched the gray between the ears. "Some Comanche or Kiowa warrior sure spent a lot of time with you." Morgan picked up the horse's left front leg, pulled his mane gently toward him, and whispered, "Down Ebon, down." The horse quickly dropped to the ground and lay on his side. Morgan knelt beside him and soothed, "Thatta boy. Good boy." He then walked several paces away from him; the horse didn't move. Morgan whistled softly again, and Ebon got up and walked quietly to him. He chuckled, "We make a pair, don't we?"

Morgan ate two of the biscuits and some beef jerky and washed them down with a long drink from the canteen. His thoughts bounced back and forth from Jubal Carver to Dog Bark, Bear Paw, and McEachern. He screwed the cap back onto the canteen, thinking, "This is where I belong…free…no people. I know why th' Kiowa didn't want to give this up, and

I don't blame him. All of this land was his—theirs—before we came...damn shame."

Morgan checked and cleaned his pistols and the Winchester. He left the camp to reconnoiter the area, and found a good spot to set a rabbit snare, thinking, "Be dark soon...I want to know for sure what's around me. Might come in handy if I have to leave in a hurry." He circled the camp, filing away in his mind the best routes to follow in case the need arose.

It was almost dark when Morgan returned to the camp; he utilized the remaining minutes of light to secure the camp. He placed his saddle and the rest of his gear beside a fallen tree and spread his poncho and blanket on the ground. The saddle would be his pillow, and the poncho and blanket his bed and cover. Morgan leaned the Winchester and Sharps against the fallen tree next to his saddle. He took the extra six-shooter from his saddlebags and placed it on the poncho, unbuckled his gun belt, and placed it there also. As was his habit when sleeping outdoors, Morgan slept with the pistol in his hand and his boots on.

He surveyed all that he had done and lay down, wrapping himself in the blanket. He looked at the cloudless sky, thinking, "It's not gonna rain. It might be better if it would...wash away my tracks." Although he hadn't seen anyone or anything to arouse his suspicions, that thought—and the fact that he had decided to run a cold camp—began to worry him. Morgan thought back to everything that had happened since he had left Fort Worth. After a while he mused to himself, "I've been as careful as I know how." He looked at Ebon, who was cropping grass nearby, and added, "He'll hear anybody way before I do." With that thought, Morgan pulled his hat over his face and went to sleep.

About an hour before daylight, Morgan opened his eyes; something or someone had awakened him. He lay perfectly still for several minutes, listening again for the sound that woke him. There it was again! Morgan slowly pushed the brim of his hat up with the barrel of his gun and looked in the direction of the sound. Ebon grazed quietly. At that moment he heard the sound again and noticed that the gelding never looked up. Morgan smiled and thought, "Whatever it is, it belongs here…most likely a deer or a coon on the way to water."

Morgan got up and walked quietly around the camp, stretching his legs and arms as he walked, still holding the Colt six-shooter in his right hand. Morgan stuck the pistol in the waistband of his trousers and retrieved his Bowie knife from his gun belt, then walked quietly toward the spot where he had set the snare. Halfway there, he stopped and relieved himself, thinking, "Roast rabbit'll sure taste good."

Morgan waited over an hour after the sun came up before he started the small fire to cook the rabbit and make coffee. He chose a spot under a wide cedar for the fire. He knew that the small amount of smoke from the short, dry pieces of wood would disperse gradually as it filtered up and through the tree. Morgan also knew that only someone close and with keen eyes could detect the smoke. After eating his fill, he sat quietly by the dying fire, drinking the last of the coffee.

Morgan retrieved the arrowhead that he had found while digging the hole for the fire and thought, "I wonder how many times this site has been used before?" He studied the gray flint arrowhead some more and answered his own question. "Many, many times. If it's a good site now, it was then too." The thought caused Morgan to conjure up images of Indians of long ago setting around a fire. He could see them laughing as they ate roasted wild game in the very spot in which he now sat. The thoughts and images caused Morgan to feel warm inside, and he sat looking into the fire for a long while.

Morgan's mind returned to the matters at hand; he took out his notebook and reviewed what he had written. Then he did what he always did in the early morning; he practiced drawing the Colt, right-handed, then left-handed. Morgan checked the rifles and began to break camp. He covered the fire first with stones and then with four or five inches of dirt, then proceeded to bury everything that would indicate that he had been here.

Morgan rode from the camp, thinking, "If things go right, I should make th' Brazos by mid-day tomorrow." He saddled up, led Ebon to the creek, and refilled his canteen while Ebon drank his fill. Morgan looked all around before he lay prone and drank from the creek. After his thirst was quenched, Morgan rode back to where he had crossed the main trail to Fort Griffin. He turned onto the trail and rode west until he saw an outcropping of hard shale to the right of the trail. Morgan continued west on the hard surface until it petered out, then rode slowly toward the Brazos and Fort Griffin, stopping frequently to watch his backtrail.

The Texas sun was high overhead when Morgan stopped in the shade of a tall cottonwood on the south side of the main Fort Griffin trail. "Quarter past twelve," he said as he checked his watch, then swung down from the horse. Morgan slapped Ebon playfully on the rump. "I'm hungry. How about you?" The gelding immediately began to crop grass. Morgan took his Winchester, canteen, and the remainder of the rabbit to the foot of the cottonwood and sat down.

Morgan ate the meat, thinking, "It's quiet…too quiet. Haven't seen very many animals either…strange." As he drank from the canteen, he thought, "I guess they're shying away from the main trail, and us…I can't say as I blame 'em." He climbed back in the saddle and continued his journey.

Morgan rode on alternate sides of the trail until about an hour before sundown; he then rode a wide circle around the trail, searching for signs of men and horses. He saw none and decided to camp for the night in a grove of trees that were located several hundred yards to the north of the traveled path.

At dusk, Morgan decided on risking a small fire; he thought, "Haven't seen any signs…camp can't be seen from the trail…only th' Kiowa could…" He dismissed that thought and started building the fire.

He had finished his meal of jerky and biscuits and was on his second cup of coffee when he heard Ebon snort. Morgan dropped the cup and drew his gun in one quick motion; he crouched and looked at Ebon. The gelding's head was up, and his ears were pointed west. Morgan moved quickly away from the fire and got behind a small boulder. He waited there for several minutes, listening and watching Ebon. He knew the horse's action would tell him what he needed to know.

Ebon nickered softly just as a man's voice called out. "Hello in th' camp."

Morgan thought, "At least it ain't th' Kiowa." He remained silent and pondered the situation.

The voice came again, "Hello in th' camp. Anybody there?" The caller waited several seconds and called out once more, "I don't mean no harm. Don't shoot. I'm comin' in."

The stranger rode slowly to the edge of the camp and stopped. He held up both hands and said, "I ain't lookin' for no trouble…just company and coffee."

Morgan studied the man and horse, thinking, "I don't know him…I've never seen th' horse before. What's he doin' this far off th' trail? Maybe lookin' for me?" He raised up, thinking, "We'll find out soon enough."

Morgan saw that Ebon had gone back to grazing, and this caused him to believe that the stranger was by himself.

"I was beginnin' to think nobody was around," smiled the stranger. "Looks like we had th' same idea."

Morgan moved out from behind the boulder and walked slowly toward the man. He stopped ten paces from him and casually asked, "What idea?"

The smile on the man's face thinned some as he replied, "Of findin' a good camp away from th' main trail. I was lookin' for one when I stumbled onto yours."

Morgan studied the man for several moments. The stranger was still smiling as he looked Morgan in the eyes. Morgan thought, "He might be all right…maybe not…best way to find out is to have him here where I can keep an eye on him."

"Climb down," Morgan said. "Coffee's hot."

The stranger slid from the horse. "Hot coffee! Music to my ears." He stuck out his hand. "Ned Farkle."

Morgan shook his hand and lied, "Bob Overton, Ned." He nodded toward the fire and added, "Hope you brought a cup. I only have th' one."

Farkle grinned, "I never leave home without one." He led his horse over to a small cedar tree and tied him off, saying, "I'm obliged to you. I wasn't lookin' forward to a cold camp by my lonesome."

Morgan sipped his coffee and studied Farkle and the horse. Morgan believed a man's horse and rig said a lot about the man. "Th' mare seems well cared for. Saddle and tack appears old and uncared for, though. They seem out of place on th' horse," he said to himself. Morgan noted the lack of trail equipment and provisions. He saw only saddlebags and a blanket. Morgan mused, "Hmm, no saddle gun or canteen… odd!" He turned his attention to Farkle. "Looks to be in his late thirties, maybe early forties. Hand was soft. That hat and shirt have seen better days, and th' trousers and boots look almost worn out." A wry smile creased Morgan's face as he looked at Farkle's gun and gun belt. They looked just as out of place as the saddle and tack did on the mare, but in the opposite way. The man carried a nickel-plated Colt .44 that sported ivory grips. The belt and holster were worn but well cared for. Farkle had the holster tied down. Morgan thought, "Gunman?"

Farkle was whistling softly as he returned to the fire and Morgan; he squatted and said, "Coffee always smells better in th' open air."

"Help yourself," Morgan replied. He was holding his cup

in his left hand; he noted that Farkle held his in both hands.

Farkle took a sip from his cup. "Coffee's first rate, Bob." He paused to look at Morgan and casually added, "You said your name was Overton?"

Morgan nodded his head. "Yes."

"I knew some Overtons up in Ellsworth, Kansas. Any kin?" His voice was friendly.

"Nope," answered Morgan. He was thinking, "He seems friendly enough...kinda careless though. Most men out here won't turn their back to a stranger like he did...I wonder?"

Farkle took another drink from his cup and said. "That gray is a fine piece of horseflesh." He put his cup down on one of the rocks around the fire and continued, "Looks to be about fifteen and a half hands."

"You've got a keen eye for horses."

Farkle grinned, "I ought to. I've busted a many of 'em in my time." He turned and looked at Ebon and stated, "I make him to be...oh, six, seven years old."

"Seven," Morgan replied. He put some more small twigs on the fire, using his left hand, and casually asked, "Are you still bustin' broncs?"

"That's what I do best," chuckled Farkle. "I just finished bustin' a string for Jedd Killpatrick over at th' Kiowa Lance in Dog Bark." Morgan sensed that Farkle wanted to see his reaction to the mention of Dog Bark and the Kiowa Lance.

Morgan's face remained void of any emotion as he thought, "You ain't no horse fighter; not with hands that soft."

"Tough way to make a livin'," Morgan said.

Farkle had a puzzled expression on his face, as though he was struggling with what to say next, but he chuckled, "That's a pure fact, my friend, but, like I said, it's what I do best."

"Now I'm his *friend*," thought Morgan.

Farkle poured himself another cup of coffee. "Bob, what line of work you in?" he asked.

"This and that," replied Morgan. "Right now, I'm just driftin'. Got me a hankerin' to see California."

Farkle whistled, "California! That's a far piece from here." He sipped his coffee and continued, "How long you been on th' trail?"

Morgan didn't answer Farkle's question. Instead, he asked one of his own. "Where're you headed, Ned?" The question caught Farkle off guard, and Morgan saw a hint of apprehension creep into his eyes.

Farkle coughed and covered, "Damn, coffee went down the wrong pipe." He cleared his throat, "Me? I'm on my way to east Texas. Got word my ma's dying." He took another sip of coffee and added, "Ain't seen her in over two years."

Both men were quiet for a while. Farkle broke the uneasy silence. "I reckon you're wonderin' why I'm travelin' light."

"It crossed my mind," said Morgan. "But I make it a habit to mind my own business. 'Sides, I figured if you wanted me to know, you'd tell me."

"No reason not to tell you," grinned Farkle. "I had to leave Fort Griffin in a hurry." His grin changed to a wide smile. "Seems she forgot to tell me she was married." Farkle slapped his leg and laughed, "He had to turn sideways to get through th' door." Farkle then proceeded to tell Morgan all the details of his escape into the night, laughing all the while. Morgan didn't say a word. He just smiled and listened.

Farkle finally noticed that Morgan wasn't saying anything. He stopped in mid-sentence and asked, "Somethin' wrong?" When Morgan didn't reply right away, Farkle's face stiffened, and he asked in a voice filled with apprehension. "I ain't talkin' to th' law am I?"

Morgan smiled and lied, "That'll be th' day." He raised his eyebrows and said, "I'm givin' 'em a wide loop these days."

"Myself," grinned Farkle. With that he poured the remaining coffee from his cup on the ground and said, "Bob, I'm plumb tuckered out; I'm gonna turn in. I'll be leavin' at first light. I gotta make some miles. Might be my last chance to see Ma alive."

"See ya in the mornin'."

"Right," he said. "I hope I don't keep you awake." He winked at Morgan and chuckled, "She said I snore somethin' awful." Farkle began to unsaddled his horse. Morgan could hear him whistling softly as he unbuckled his gun belt and placed it on the saddle horn. Farkle spread his blanket on the ground and rolled himself up in it. Five minutes later he was snoring loudly.

Morgan sat by the fire looking intently at Farkle. "Th' man can snore…can't nobody pretend to snore that long and that loud. He's sure enough asleep." The truth in that thought caused Morgan to think, "Maybe I've got him wrong. He could be who and what he says he is." He thought long. "Only one thing could make a frontier man that trusting…to turn his back on a stranger he just met, and go to sleep away from his gun." Morgan's eyes were hard and pitch black as he thought, "He knows who I am!"

The sun had been up for nearly an hour when Farkle sat up and rubbed the sleep out of his eyes. Morgan was squatting by the fire, drinking coffee. "Damn," groaned Farkle. "I must be gettin' old." He grinned at Morgan and added, "And absent-minded. Pert near forgot my manners. Mornin." His eyes strayed to Ebon who was standing on the far side of the camp, saddled and ready for the trail. Morgan's gun belt and gun were hanging from the saddle horn.

"Mornin'," replied Morgan. "I didn't want to wake you, and I didn't feel right ridin' off with you still asleep."

"That's mighty kind of you, Bob. "I'm obliged to you, again." Farkle yawned and stretched as he buckled on his gun belt. Morgan saw him glance over at Ebon as he tied the holster to his leg. He was saying to the mare, "We got some hard ridin' today…gotta make up for lost time."

Morgan put his cup down, thinking, "If I was right...."

Farkle's voice stopped his thought. "Morgan! Stuart Morgan!"

Morgan looked up from the fire. Farkle had his gun in his hand; it was pointed at Morgan.

A wry smile appeared on Morgan's lips. He stared at Farkle and the gun for a moment, and then quietly said, "I was beginnin' to think you weren't gonna make your play."

Morgan's calmness and apparent unconcern for his predicament caused Farkle some concern and doubt. Farkle looked furtively again toward Ebon and Morgan's gun. He shrugged his shoulders, "I'd just about decided to give it up until..." He nodded his head toward the gelding, "you got careless."

"Ned, things aren't always as they seem. I didn't get careless." Morgan lowered his voice. "You did."

"I did, huh?" sneered Farkle; he cocked the Colt and continued, "Then why have *I* got th' gun?"

Morgan acted like he hadn't heard. "Ned, listen carefully. I'm only gonna say this one time." His voice was calm and even. "Drop th' gun, and you can ride out and live." Morgan's stern voice and calm demeanor were startling to Farkle, but only for a moment. He reasoned that he had Morgan between a rock and a hard spot.

"They said you were a cool one," laughed Farkle. He took two steps toward Morgan and added, "And you're clever too, aren't you?" He took another step and continued, "Morgan, you know what I think?" Farkle's face blanked as his eyes got big and wide. "I think you made a big mistake, and you're tryin' to talk your way out of it."

"Suit yourself," sighed Morgan. "But there's somethin' you oughtta know."

"I know," chuckled Farkle. "There's someone behind me."

Morgan shook his head, "You've got enough trouble with th' man in front of you." Morgan saw doubt reappear in

Farkle's eyes and face once again.

Farkle snarled, "End of conversation. You've been bought and paid for. I—"

Morgan interrupted. "One more thing—"

"What now?" snapped Farkle.

Morgan smiled faintly. "I've got my spare Colt tucked in my waistband…behind." He pointed behind him.

Farkle laughed out loud, "Morgan, you beat all. You know it?" He holstered his gun and said, "You're too good of a man to die like this." He nodded his head toward Morgan's horse and pistol. "I'm gonna count to three. Maybe you can get there; maybe not; or maybe, I'll miss."

Morgan didn't reply; he stood and stared at Farkle.

"I know it's a shitty deal," said Farkle. "But it's th' only deal you're gonna get this day."

After several seconds, Morgan broke the eerie silence. In a whisper that sounded like a shout, he said, "Ned, I took th' shells from your gun while you slept last night."

Morgan's words caused Farkle to slightly tremble as he thought about Morgan's latest revelation, but he quickly regained his composure and confidence. He chuckled, "Time to fish or cut bait, Morgan." He grinned, starting to count. "One…two…" Farkle drew his gun on the count of two as did Morgan.

Morgan was watching Farkle's eyes as the hammer of his Colt struck the empty chamber. The loud, empty click sent shocked disbelief to his eyes and terror to his face. Morgan's gun barked an instant later. The impact of the slug sent Farkle reeling backwards. Farkle took one halting step forward and sat down hard. He was still holding the empty gun when Morgan walked to him.

Farkle looked up at Morgan and then back to his gun. Death was already in his eyes; he whispered, "How? I didn't believe you…" His voice faded away.

Morgan held out his left hand and opened his fist; six cartridges fell to the ground between Farkle's legs. Morgan squatted in front of Farkle. "Ned, you said they told you I was cool and clever."

Farkle was dying, and he knew it. He coughed. Blood trickled from the corner of his mouth, and he tried unsuccessfully to lick it away as he feebly whispered, "They…Woodson …and…." His eyes closed as he slumped over onto his right side and died.

Morgan took the gun from Farkle's lifeless hand. "Ned, they should've told you somethin' else about me. I don't lie."

Chapter Four

Morgan turned Farkle's mare loose, thinking, "Somebody'll pick her up. She'd just slow me down, and I need to get movin'. Sound of gunshot carries. If anybody's close…bound to have heard it." Morgan returned to Farkle's body and hurriedly searched it, hoping to find some clue that could tell him more about whoever had sent him, but he didn't find anything. He did however find two gold double eagles. He thought, "Forty dollars. A man's life ain't worth much these days." Morgan searched Farkle's saddlebags with the same result; he found two more gold double eagles and thought, "Eighty dollars…still ain't much for a man's life." He found nothing else of interest.

Morgan dragged Farkle's body over to a cluster of small boulders and wedged him between them. He placed Farkle's saddle and his gear on top of the body and covered everything with brush that he had hurriedly cut with his hatchet. Morgan added stones, thinking, "Ned, I ain't got time to give you a decent burial even if I was of a mind to." He placed the last rock on the make-shift grave and added, "Which I ain't."

Morgan followed Farkle's tracks for several hundred yards and stopped in a stand of cedar trees. He waited to see if anyone would investigate his shot. Morgan patted Ebon on the neck and whispered, "Ebon, I can't shake th' feelin' that Farkle wasn't playin' a lone hand. We'll sit a spell."

He took out his notebook and reviewed what McEachern had told him. Morgan replaced the notebook in his shirt pocket, thinking, "Farkle said 'Woodson and' just before he died." Morgan frowned at the thought and mused, "Karl Woodson? Maybe…he could've wired…he knew where I was headed. Farkle said 'and'…if it was Karl…wonder who he wired? Easy enough to check out."

Morgan watched for over an hour without seeing or hearing anyone. He rode quietly out of the cedars and picked up Farkle's trail again; it led him to the main trail where it turned west toward Fort Griffin. Morgan stopped and studied the situation. "Well, he didn't follow me from Fort Worth… most likely came from Griffin or Dog Bark."

High noon found Morgan some ten miles from the Brazos, sitting on a log, eating jerky and the last of the biscuits. He'd made poor time because of his reluctance to ride the main trail and because he'd paused several times to watch his backtrail. Morgan drank from the canteen, thinking, "One or two days ain't gonna make no difference. Everything'll still be there…McEachern said 'end of June'." Morgan smiled at the thought as he climbed back on Ebon and continued west.

Morgan was less than a mile from the Brazos when he saw

the circling vultures up ahead. He thought, "Buzzards! What now? A bunch of 'em…must be somethin' big to attract that many." He continued on cautiously knowing that whatever or whoever had drawn the scavengers was most likely beyond his help. He would take his time and size up the situation.

Morgan stopped in a shallow ravine, thinking, "Whatever they're after should be just over this bank." He took his rifle and field glasses and quietly crawled to the rim of the embankment. Once there, he took off his hat and lay prone in the underbrush and grass. Morgan saw immediately what had drawn the vultures; through field glasses he studied the two bodies sprawled on the river bank below and thought, "Somebody's luck has run out. Men…too far away to make 'em out…they're sure enough dead though."

After checking the area several times with the field glasses, Morgan reasoned that whoever killed the men had long since departed. He crawled down the embankment, thinking, "Road agents? Maybe Farkle? Naw, he was with me." Morgan climbed onto Ebon, rubbed the gelding's neck and said aloud, "Ebon, keep your ears open. This may not be what it appears to be."

Morgan rode slowly toward the two men, ever alert for movement or sound. With the Winchester cocked and ready, he stopped twenty yards from where the men lay and scanned the area again, but he saw nothing to alarm him. However, he picked out an escape route to take in the event of trouble.

Morgan knew a dead man when he saw one. He was still ten yards from the first man when he said, "Buzzard's already been vistin'." He noted that the man was face down in what had been a campfire. Morgan gently pulled the dead man from the ashes and turned him over. Although the man's face was badly burned, Morgan recognized him immediately. He squatted beside the man and quietly asked, "Pete, who cut your throat?" Morgan thought for a moment and answered his own question. "Bear Paw!"

The other body was lying on a blanket, some ten yards from the campfire. Morgan walked over, thinking, "Wherever you find Pete, you'll find Burl." Burl Gistinger was face up with his eyes open. Like Pete, his throat had been cut. Morgan squatted beside him and noted that he had also been scalped. Morgan closed Burl's eyelids and sighed, "Burl, we were both wrong. You ain't gonna piss on my grave, and you ain't gonna end up six feet under, 'cause I ain't got the time or the notion." Morgan pulled the blanket from under Burl, covered him with it, and added, "Even if I did, the earth would vomit you back up."

Morgan pulled Pete next to Burl and covered him with the other blanket. He searched the area and discovered three sets of prints. Morgan studied the moccasin print and thought, "It could be him, but maybe not." He stood back and surveyed the camp again, thinking, "I figure it was early this mornin' when he jumped 'em. Burl was asleep, and Pete was by th' fire…most likely took Pete first. Bet they never heard him."

Morgan circled the camp until he found where whoever was wearing the moccasins had entered. He also found the place where Burl and Pete had tied their horses for the night. He pondered the situation a bit longer, "He was only interested in th' guns and horses." An image of the Kiowa's face that day at Medicine Lodge caused Morgan to shiver as he added, "And killin'."

Morgan went through the dead men's pockets, but found nothing that answered any of his questions. He covered them again, thinking, "If they'd wanted to bushwhack me…why this far from Fort Worth? Maybe they and Woodson…someone in Dog Bark?"

The moccasin tracks were easy to follow and caused Morgan to think. "Ain't like an Indian to be this careless." Morgan frowned and said, "Unless he wants you to follow." The tracks led Morgan to where the killer had tied his horse.

What he found there startled him at first, then sent shivers throughout his body. Someone had drawn a crude bear print in the dirt and left an arrow sticking in the middle of it.

Morgan cocked the Winchester and thought, "Bear Paw!" He stared at the arrow only briefly and was immediately on the alert, looking all around, listening, thinking, "It's him all right. I've seen that arrow before…at Medicine Lodge. He wants me to find it. That's why he left the tracks. I wonder how long he's been watchin' me? If he'd wanted to kill me, he'd have tried by now. Only other explanation is that he hasn't seen me…left the arrow for anybody to find." Morgan thought back to that day at Medicine Lodge and the day in '68 in the buffalo wallow; he visualized the Kiowa's face and eyes and mused, "No, he knows it's me. I wonder what he's got planned?"

Morgan took the arrow and slowly started to follow the sign; it took him back to the Gistingers' camp where the rider took Burl's and Pete's horses. He followed them, thinking, "I was right. Tracks are ten, twelve hours old. One unshod, two shod."

Morgan was better than most at tracking and following sign, but he knew he was at a considerable disadvantage when it came to an Indian such as Bear Paw. He rubbed Ebon's neck and said aloud, "Ebon, he's headed north, and he ain't in no hurry." Morgan studied the tracks a while longer and added, "We're goin' west."

Nightfall found Morgan eight miles west of the Brazos, camped in the bottom of a dry creek bed. A fire hadn't even entered his mind; he sat in the dark eating jerky, thinking, "I've done all I know how. If he's followin', he'll come in right at daybreak." The faint sound of thunder caused Morgan to look northwest; he saw lightning and thought, "I hope that storm blows in before mornin'. Make it hard to follow sign; even for him, I hope."

The thunderstorm hit at four-thirty just as Morgan reached

the main trail; he turned Ebon west and thought, "Gotta make as many miles as I can. Hope this rain lasts. I'd rather be wet than dead." He pulled his hat lower and turned up his collar and said, "Ebon, we got us some ridin' to do. Dry livery and oats are waitin' at Griffin." The gelding seemed to understand; he broke into a brisk trot as Morgan smiled and thought, "I could use some grub and a dry bed myself."

Chapter Five

Stuart Morgan rode into the Fort Griffin Livery and Stable just as the sun was setting. He stripped the saddle from the gray, led him into an empty stall, and began rubbing him down with dry hay. "I'll wire Marshall Reynolds in th' mornin'...let him know about Burl and Pete. I'm bone tired and hungry as a bear...I wonder if there's a place I can get a hot bath?" He closed the stall gate as a stranger walked up and peered into the stall.

The man looked at Ebon for several moments and turned to Morgan. "Mighty fine lookin' horse you got there, stranger. What's his name?"

Morgan nodded his head. "I call him Ebon."

"Ebon?" repeated the man as he looked Morgan up and down. "You come in from Dog Bark?"

"Nope." Morgan's voice was friendly.

The stranger looked quizzically at Morgan as though he were expecting him to tell him more. After several moments of silence, he said, "Uh-huh." He then went back to the stall, looked at Ebon, and announced, "Feller up at Fort Sill has a horse that looks like your'n." He sucked his teeth and added, "He calls him Twister. 'Course he's a stud." He sauntered back over to where Morgan was getting his gear together and asked, "Concho, right?"

Morgan slung the saddlebags over his shoulder and smiled, "No."

The man scratched his head and frowned, "You don't talk much, do you?"

Morgan looked around the livery, then turned to the stranger, "Livery man around?"

The man grinned, "You're lookin' at him." He stuck out his hand, "Asa Whitmore."

Morgan took his hand and said, "Stuart Morgan. How much for the horse?"

"Two bits...includes hay and oats." He was thinking, "Stuart Morgan? Where've I heard that name?"

Morgan gave Whitmore fifty cents. "See that he gets a double ration of oats."

Asa pocketed the coin and said, "Only decent place in town to eat is Wasserman's lunch room." He followed Morgan to the door and added, "If you're hankerin' for a hot bath..." He smiled as Morgan turned around and continued, "Kelly's Barber Shop." He nodded his head to the right, "Next to the general store."

Morgan walked back to Whitmore with a wry smile on his face and asked, "Asa, is there anything else I need to know?"

Whitmore smiled back, "Bed bugs'll carry you off over at

th' hotel." He nodded toward the loft. "Be a heap quieter up there, too…you could keep an eye on th' gray." Asa's smile widened, "Same as th' horse. Two bits."

Morgan was thinking, "Every town has one. Maybe he can be of use." He fished a quarter from his pocket, tossed it to Whitmore, and asked, "Anything else on your mind?"

Whitmore looked first at the Colt on Morgan's hip and then to the two rifles he was holding and said in a serious voice, "Sheriff's name is Tom Dobby. If I wuz you, I'd check in with him. He don't cotton to gunfighters much." He saw the frown that appeared on Morgan's face and quickly added, "No offense intended."

Morgan's frown changed to a grin, "None taken. Sounds like good advice." He handed the rifles to Whitmore and added, "Keep an eye on these 'til I get back. Th' Winchester's loaded."

Whitmore followed Morgan outside and called after him, "Wichita Falls, right?" Morgan shook his head and kept walking. Whitmore watched Morgan some more and mused to himself, "A man's got to be from somewhere." He scratched the stubble on his cheek and said, "Maybe El Paso…or Fort Sill."

After taking a hot bath and eating a steak, Morgan returned to the livery; he checked on Ebon and climbed the ladder to the loft, thinking, "The soldier at th' lunchroom said he'd tell Coldiron I was here. Maybe Coldiron'll know what's goin' on at Dog Bark…have information on Carver…th' Kiowa. I wanna be on th' trail to Dog Bark by noon. I'll send a wire to Reynolds, check in with Sheriff Dobby."

Morgan smiled as he saw that someone had spread fresh hay in the loft and left a blanket for him; his rifles were on the blanket. Morgan checked the two rifles, thinking, "Seems I've got a friend in Whitmore."

Although he was dead tired, Morgan checked and cleaned

his two pistols and went through his practice routine, both right and left-handed. He unbuckled his gun belt and thought, "I'm almost there...can't tell much difference. A little more practice oughtta do it."

Morgan pulled the blanket over him, knowing Ebon would alert him if anyone entered the livery; he palmed the Colt and went to sleep to dream of Farkle, Devlin, the Kiowa, Jubal Carver, and his father.

As usual, Morgan was up before sunrise. He gave Ebon hay and oats then went to Wasserman's for breakfast. Morgan was halfway through his eggs and bacon when a tall, thin man came in and walked directly to him. Morgan moved his fork to his left hand and continued eating, never looking at the man.

"You Stuart Morgan?"

Morgan looked up, "Who's askin'?"

The stranger pulled aside his vest to reveal the badge pinned to his shirt pocket. "Deputy Collins."

Morgan looked at the badge and then back into Collins' eyes. "I'm Morgan."

Collins covered the badge, "Sheriff Dobby'd like a word with you."

Morgan was thinking, "Asa's been busy." He took a sip of his coffee and replied, "Tell him I'll be along."

Collins studied slowly and carefully; Morgan stared back in much the same manner. Finally, the deputy nodded his head, turned, and slowly walked away.

Morgan finished his meal, got a shave at Kelly's, and sent a wire to Reynolds. He sauntered toward the Sheriff's office, thinking, "Word travels fast; both th' barber and telegrapher knew my name...I wonder what else Asa told 'em? Dobby's gonna tell me to move on." He smiled wryly at the last thought and mused inwardly, "I've told a few to move on myself."

Morgan entered the sheriff's office and found Dobby at his desk going through a stack of 'wanted' posters. Collins was seated at a desk with his feet propped up. Morgan went to Dobby and stopped right in front of his desk. Dobby continued to go through the posters, giving no indication that he knew Morgan was there. The only sound in the office was the shuffling of the posters.

Collins broke the silence. "He says he's Stuart Morgan."

"I not only say, I *am* Stuart Morgan." Morgan's tone was firm but casual. Dobby looked up at Morgan briefly and began shuffling through the 'wanted' posters again, which prompted Morgan to add, "I'll save you th' trouble. I ain't wanted."

Dobby put down the posters and asked, "Morgan, what brings you to Fort Griffin?"

"Just passin' through on my way to Dog Bark."

Dobby's eyes hadn't left Morgan's; he put his hands behind his head and said, "Morgan! Th' name's familiar." He leaned forward and continued, "Th' Stuart Morgan I know of was with MacKenzie, and th' last I heard, was workin' for Reynolds up in Fort Worth."

"I heard that Morgan killed Frank Devlin," interrupted Collins; his voice was thick with sarcasm.

Morgan's face remained void of emotion, and his tone remained casual. "You're both right, on all accounts."

"I've had some dealin's with Reynolds before," Dobby said. "How's the big redhead doin'?"

Morgan smiled, "We ain't talkin' about th' same man."

Dobby smiled for the first time. "No, I reckon we ain't at that." He rose and stuck out his hand, "Tom Dobby, Stuart."

Morgan shook Dobby's hand, thinking, "I gotta be careful; I don't want to ask too many questions or say th' wrong thing."

"I was on my way over here when your deputy…." He cut his eyes toward Collins as his voice faded.

Dobby chuckled, "I'm sorry 'bout that. Just tryin' to head off trouble 'fore it starts." He grinned and continued, "Listen to me. Hell, you've been there. We've had more hardcases through here of late. It's become a full-time job runnin' 'em out of town."

Collins licked the paper of a cigarette he was making and commented, "Dog Bark's a little ways out of your jurisdiction, ain't it?"

"I'm not a lawman right now," replied Morgan. "I'm hopin' to get on at Dog Bark."

"I ain't one to tell someone his business," Dobby said. "But if it was me, I'd stay clear of that mess; all hell's breakin' loose down there."

"So I've heard," replied Morgan.

"Luther Piper's the sheriff there," said Dobby. "He a friend of yours?"

"Never met th' man. He and Nolan Reynolds are old friends. I'm doin' it as a favor to Nolan."

"Piper's needin' a deputy all right," laughed Collins.

Dobby frowned at Collins, then said to Morgan, "Two of Piper's deputies were killed several months ago, and another one has disappeared."

"Still want th' job?" quipped Collins.

Morgan acted as though he hadn't heard Collins, took a piece of paper from his shirt pocket, and handed it to Dobby. "There's three dead men back on th' trail to Fort Worth." Morgan pointed to the paper and added, "I've drawn a map of th' approximate locations of their bodies."

"Three dead men!" exclaimed Collins.

Dobby looked at the map for a moment. "You kill 'em?"

"Only one of 'em," answered Morgan; then he told Dobby about Ned Farkle and how he'd found Burl and Pete. Morgan finished by saying, "I wired Marshall Reynolds this mornin'. I wasn't sure about jurisdiction."

By now Collins was standing next to Dobby. "What'd Farkle look like?" After Morgan had described him, Collins said, "That's Farkle all right. Ned was better'n a fair hand with a gun." He raised his eyebrows and added, "And you beat him?" His tone was unbelieving.

Morgan's eyes turned pitch black, and his face stiffened as he said evenly, "I did." He stared at Collins until the latter looked away and added, "Farkle was a fool." He paused for a moment as though he was thinking, "So was Frank Devlin."

There was a period of uneasy silence among the three men. Dobby cleared his throat, "I ran Farkle's sorry ass outta here in January. I heard he was at Dog Bark." He scratched his chin and continued, "And that's kinda strange. Piper don't normally let his sort stay long. Any idea who sicked Farkle on you?"

Morgan shook his head, "He only said I'd been bought and paid for."

"If it's any help, Ned played poker on occasions at Blackthorn with Freeman Burkett and Carl Zachary," said Dobby. "Burkett's a gambler. Zachary's a puncher for Jedd Killpatrick."

Morgan reflected on what Dobby had told him. "Dobby seems all right, but I'm not so sure about Collins." He stuck out his hand to Dobby, "Thanks for th' information. I'm obliged."

Dobby shook Morgan's hand. "Sure thing. Good luck to you."

Morgan was halfway to the door when Collins called after him. "Are you sure those other two birds were killed by that renegade Comanche?"

Morgan turned to Collins, "Yeah, I'm sure they were killed, but not by no Comanche. They were killed by a Kiowa named Bear Paw." Morgan continued to stare at Collins.

The deputy finally sputtered, "If Coldiron and the damned army'd get off their sorry asses—"

"Captain Coldiron's a friend of mine," interrupted Morgan. He smiled wryly at Collins and said to Dobby, "Thanks again, Tom. Be seein' ya."

As soon as Morgan closed the door, Collins said, "He don't look like much to me. Hell, he's dressed like…no way he's faster'n Devlin…or Farkle." Collins drew his pistol, spun the cylinder, twirled it, and deftly returned it to his holster.

"Son, you got a lot to learn," sighed Dobby.

"He don't scare me none."

Dobby chuckled, "He don't, huh?"

"Hell no," smirked Collins. He drew his gun again and added, "I'm twice as fast as Farkle was."

Dobby deadpanned, "Not only have you got a lot to learn…" Dobby lowered his voice and continued, "You're like an owl."

"An owl?" asked Collins.

By now Dobby was at the door; he opened it and said, "Yeah, an owl. Th' more light that's shined on you, th' less you see."

Morgan arrived at the livery to find Coldiron talking to Ebon. Coldiron was saying, "Ebon, worst mistake I ever made was givin' you to Morgan." He winked at Ebon as he heard Morgan coming up behind him. "You're way too smart for—" He turned and smiled at Morgan and finished his sentence, "Stuart Morgan."

Chapter Six

Morgan and Captain Burt Coldiron talked quietly for nearly two hours. It was always the same when they met; they talked of past Indian campaigns, of their days with MacKenzie, of Medicine Lodge, and, as usual, they ended up rehashing the Palo Duro attack and the subsequent slaughtering of the Comanche and Kiowa horse herds.

"What's done is done," sighed Coldiron. "Wasn't mine or your doin' no how, Stuart; put it to rest. Leave it lay."

"Wasn't right," said Morgan. His tone was somber.

"Maybe not, but there ain't nothin' or nobody gonna change what's been done."

Morgan stepped across the livery to his belongings and got

the arrow Bear Paw had left at the murder site and handed it to Coldiron. "We got one out there who ain't lettin' it lay."

Coldiron studied the arrow for a moment and frowned, "Kiowa?"

"I'm glad to see you ain't forgot everything I taught you," smiled Morgan. Then he filled Coldiron in on how he had found Burl and Pete and the arrow. Morgan omitted the account of the episode with Farkle.

Coldiron whistled softly, "Kiowa! We've...I thought..." His thoughts raced so that his voice couldn't keep up.

"Your renegade's a Kiowa named Bear Paw."

Coldiron passed the arrow back to Morgan. "Bear Paw...Bear Paw. Where've I heard that name?"

Morgan stared at some faraway point in space as he quietly replied, "'67. Medicine Lodge. He was th' last to speak. I can still see his face, remember his words. He said, 'From where I now stand, until th' sun and th' moon are no more...even when th' wolf is in my belly, I, Bear Paw of th' Kiowa Nation, will eat dung or starve rather than travel th' white man's road. These are my words.'"

Coldiron snapped his fingers, "Of course! Now I remember." He again took the arrow from Morgan and drew a crude print of a bears' paw with the arrow, "When he finished talkin' he did this." Coldiron stuck the arrow in the middle of the paw print he had drawn.

Morgan nodded his head in agreement. "I remember...both arrows identical—black with three red circles." He paused, lowered his voice, and added, "Th' man's carryin' a lot of hatred, Burt. He's gonna raise a lot of hell 'fore he's through. You're gonna have to have a lot of luck to catch him."

"We ain't had much luck so far," Coldiron sighed. "Hell, Stuart, he's a shadow, a puff of smoke. First, he's here, then a day later, he's in Oklahoma—then Kansas. Ain't no way one man, even if he's an Indian—"

"One thing you can be sure of," interrupted Morgan. "He's out there, and he ain't through raisin' hell. Burt, I gotta feelin' he's just gettin' started."

"I could get you on as a scout again. Me and you together could—"

Morgan cut him off firmly with a hint of a smile, "I've gotta look into that situation at Dog Bark I told you about." He began saddling Ebon and added, "I'm not sure I want to be th' one…to kill him, even if I could." He turned to Coldiron and added, "Burt, I'm not even sure I have th' skill, much less th' stomach for it."

Coldiron frowned, "Down deep you don't believe he's doin' wrong, do you?"

"Burt, it really doesn't matter what I think." Morgan's face went dead, and his voice sounded tired as he continued. "You wanna know why, Burt?" Before Coldiron could reply, Morgan continued. "It's long past th' point of right or wrong. Besides, it's what Bear Paw thinks that matters."

Coldiron sighed, "Is this gonna be another one of your poor, mistreated Indian speeches?"

Morgan's eyes found Coldirons'. "Burt, he's only doin' what he's been raised and trained all his life to do. He's at war with people who killed his family…kin, and almost his whole tribe. We destroyed his way of life."

Coldiron gazed into Morgan's eyes for a moment. He shook his head and smiled, "Arguin' with you is like tryin' to piss up a wet rope."

"Wasn't arguin'," said Morgan. "I was just havin' my say." As he swung his leg over Ebon, he added in a concerned tone. "Burt, you be real careful—"

Coldiron reached up and took Morgan's hand and chuckled. "You can count on it." He winked at Morgan and added, "Future generals don't make mistakes." He clasped Morgan's hand, "Watch your back. Those people at Dog Bark make th' renegade look like a Sunday school teacher."

Morgan grinned, "I aim to. Be seein' ya."

Coldiron watched Morgan ride off and thought, "Ol' pard, you'll never understand—they were doomed from th' get go, and that's th' plain truth."

Asa Whitmore came out of the livery and sidled up to Coldiron. "Interestin' fella, that Morgan. He a friend of yours?"

Coldiron didn't reply right away, and when he did, he spoke as though he was unaware of Whitmore's presence. "You should've seen us at Palo Duro. God a'mighty, we were somethin'—"

On the way out of Fort Griffin, Morgan stopped at the general store and bought a two-day supply of grub. About a mile out, he doubled back east of the trail, found a secluded spot, and stopped. After waiting for awhile, Morgan checked his watch and said, "Ebon, guess I was wrong. Let's go get our package."

Morgan rode back to the place where he had stashed his badge, letter of appointment, the four gold pieces, and Farkle's gun. Upon arriving, he studied the area for any sign that his hiding place had been discovered, but he found nothing to arouse his suspicions.

He had just placed the items in his saddlebags when Ebon's ears came up. Morgan reacted immediately; he grabbed the Winchester, slapped the gelding on the rump and dove head first over a fallen tree. While in mid-air, he felt something slam into his left foot; then he heard the gunshot.

Morgan rolled quickly to his left, thinking, "Rifle, hundred yards at least...who? Th' Kiowa?" It dawned on him that he felt no pain in his left foot. Looking at his boot he saw the slug had only knocked the heel off. He thought, "Piece of luck there. I can't stay pinned down here...could be more'n one of 'em. If it's Bear Paw, he won't stay in one place; he'll be circlin' soon. I'll stand a better chance goin' after him."

Morgan peeped over the tree and quickly lowered his head; his movement brought another shot. The bullet gouged a chunk of bark and wood inches from where his head had been. He rolled over twice to his right and fired at the brush from where the shot had come and moved quickly back to his left as another shot rang out. Morgan jacked a cartridge into the chamber and thought, "Whoever it is, he can shoot." He scanned behind him and to his left and right but saw nothing alarming. "Only one bushwhacker, I think…time to move."

Morgan belly-crawled to the end of the fallen tree, and then quickly into the brush and grass. He continued crawling Indian-style for about twenty yards before he stopped and carefully parted the brush. When he caught a glimpse of someone moving quickly away, Morgan brought the rifle up, but he was too late. The ambusher had disappeared behind a clump of trees. Seconds later Morgan heard the sounds of a running horse.

Morgan lay where he was for several minutes pondering his situation, and then quietly began working his way toward the spot where the shots had originated. When he arrived there, he found several puzzling things. Whoever had fired at him was wearing moccasins but riding a shod horse. Morgan studied the prints, thinking, "Odd. Still, it might be th' Kiowa." He pictured the prints he'd found at the site where Burl and Pete had been killed and mused, "No, it's not him. These are too small. A white man wearin' moccasins?"

Further examination of the area turned up four shell casings. Morgan put them in his pocket and thought, "He only fired three times…why four casings? He's careful; carries an empty under th' pin."

Morgan whistled for Ebon and resumed his journey to Dog Bark. The attempt on his life caused him to be careful in the extreme; he rode both sides of the main trail, stopped often, and doubled back several times to see if the bushwhacker was following, all of which caused him to make poor time. Although Morgan wasn't concerned about time, he was concerned with staying alive and therefore didn't begrudge the time spent on being cautious.

Morgan reached Blackthorn with nearly two hours of daylight remaining, and although it was only twelve miles to Dog Bark, he had already made up his mind not to push on. Morgan circled Blackthorn and rode until dusk. He found a secluded campsite and bedded down for the night.

The next morning found Morgan halfway to Dog Bark as the sun peeked over the horizon. He had spent a restless night trying to piece together and understand all that had happened since he had left Fort Worth. Morgan rubbed Ebons' neck. "Ebon, I reckon it'll sort itself out." He took a bite of jerky and added, "One thing is certain…someone's makin' it plain. We ain't welcome in Dog Bark."

Morgan checked his watch and thought, "Should be in Dog Bark 'bout noon. Today's th' seventeenth; McEachern should arrive at Fort Griffin today or tomorrow. Maybe he can find out where Woodson is. Why would he go to all this trouble? Doesn't figure, but Farkle plainly said 'Woodson.' Burl and Pete, I can understand. Th' four of 'em workin' together? Seems unlikely…and who was th' gent in moccasins? Bear Paw? Jubal Carver? Where does he fit in? and Piper? Only person left…" Morgan frowned. "Mac? Not likely…he ain't got th' guts." Morgan's thoughts were interrupted by the sound of an approaching horse.

Morgan was riding some fifty yards or so off the main trail; he guided Ebon behind a stand of trees, took out his field glasses, and waited for the rider to pass. Morgan studied the rider for several moments. "Collins…th' deputy from Fort Griffin! What's he doin' at Dog Bark?" Morgan answered his first question with another. "Tellin' someone I was on my way?"

Morgan watched Collins until he was out of sight and started for Dog Bark, thinking, "Where does a deputy sheriff from Griffin fit into this? Maybe he was sent by Dobby...maybe not."

After Morgan left the stand of trees, another horse and rider slipped from behind a large clump of trees and brush some forty yards away. It was Bear Paw.

Chapter Seven

Sweat trickled down Morgan's spine as he gazed at Dog Bark for the first time. He'd just climbed down from a big, live oak tree where he had stashed his badge and the letter of appointment. Wiping the sweat from his brow, he patted Ebon's neck. "Ebon, it looks plumb peaceful, don't it?" Ebon shook his head and nickered softly. Morgan chuckled, "You don't believe it?" He urged Ebon forward as he added, "Me neither."

Morgan rode slowly toward Dog Bark, thinking, "I'm gonna look around first…get th' feel of things. Maybe someone'll tip their hand. I'll see Piper tomorrow. Gotta get Ebon settled in. It's a good time to have his shoes checked;

hell, I'll get a heel put on my boot. If Carver's here, I don't wanna spook him. Gonna need some time to smoke him out."

Dog Bark's main street ran north and south. Morgan read the signs as he rode slowly toward the livery at the south end of the street; Farquar's General Store, Dog Bark Clarion, O'Banion, M.D., Gunsmith, Telegraph, County Sheriff, Wes Tankersley—Attorney at Law, Bank, Dog Bark City Hall, Hotel, Smith's Boot & Saddle, McKown's Dry Goods, Seth's Barber Shop & Undertaker Services, One-Eyed Jack Saloon, Overland Stage Depot. Morgan stopped in front of the livery and read the sign. "Willson's Livery and Blacksmith—Kyle Willson, Proprietor."

Morgan climbed down just as a short, burly man emerged from the livery. Morgan nodded his head, "Howdy."

The man nodded his head and asked, "What can I do for you?"

"Need room and board for my horse."

The blacksmith didn't answer right away; he studied Morgan and Ebon intently for several moments and said, "All right." He turned and went back into the livery. Morgan followed. The man gestured to an empty stall. "Fifty cents a day…in advance…includes hay and oats."

Morgan led Ebon into the stall and began unsaddling. The stocky liveryman walked over and asked, "How long might you be stayin'?"

"Depends," replied Morgan. He handed the man a silver dollar and said, "I'd be obliged if you'd check his shoes."

Willson was caught up in staring at Morgan and didn't reply right away. He put the dollar in his pocket, thinking, "Just what we need, another gunfighter. Winchester and a Sharps? Killpatrick or Haggard's sure startin' to play rough." Willson finally spoke. "I'll check him out right after I eat, Mr…"

Morgan smiled wryly. "Kyle, I'm Stuart Morgan, from Fort Worth." He gathered up his belongings and walked slowly away, leaving Willson standing with a perplexed look on his face.

Willson watched Morgan until he disappeared into Smith's Boot and Saddle, then walked slowly over to Ebon's stall. He studied the gray gelding for a moment and said, "Hoss, I'm bettin' ol' Dog Bark's fixin' to liven up a mite."

The cobbler handed Morgan his boot. "Good as new. That'll be four-bits." These were the first words he had spoken since Morgan had entered his shop.

Morgan gave him two quarters and chuckled, "I've been to some unfriendly towns in my time..." Morgan let his comment trail off. He put the boot on and continued, "A stranger usually gets th' same old questions: 'What's your name? Be stayin' long? Where're you from?'"

The bootmaker pocketed the quarters then nodded his head toward the front window, and the man who was peering intently at them. "It don't matter who you are or where you're from, and you probably won't be stayin' very long." He paused, raised his eyebrows, then added, "Deputy Rideout sees to such matters."

"Is that a fact," replied Morgan, staring at the man who was peering in the window until he walked away. Turning to the bootmaker, Morgan stated, "Th' name's Morgan, Stuart Morgan. I'm from Fort Worth." He paused, looked squarely at the cobbler's eyes, smiled faintly, and added, "And I'll stay as long as I like." The bootmaker noticed Morgan's eyes had turned pitch black.

As Morgan crossed the street to the saloon, he spied the man who had watched his dealings through the window with such interest. The man was entering the livery. Morgan peered over the bat-wings, thinking, "Rideout. McEachern mentioned him. One of Piper's deputies. He's checkin' on me." Morgan stuck Farkle's six-shooter in his belt and stepped into the barroom.

All activity ceased as he entered the saloon; every head turned toward him; the place was suddenly silent. Morgan smiled to himself as he placed the Winchester and the Sharps against the wall. He neatly piled the rest of his belongings on a nearby table and walked to the bar. The only sounds he heard were those of his own making.

"Beer," said Morgan.

The bartender stood mesmerized and didn't speak right away.

Morgan leaned toward him, "You do have beer, don't you?"

The bartender found his tongue and stammered, "Right. I wuz jus'. Yes, sir...yes, we do."

"Fine," Morgan said. He was watching the five men at the poker table, who in turn were staring at him.

After several more moments of uneasy silence, one of the men said, "Ain't nobody ever seen a damn stranger before? I came here to play poker. Burkett, you gonna deal them cards or hatch 'em?"

The bartender's hand trembled as he placed a mug of beer in front of Morgan. "Beer's a nickel." He nodded his head to the end of the bar and continued, "There's bread, cheese, and meat, if you're hungry."

Morgan nodded his head "yes", took the beer, and returned to his table. Seating himself with his back to the wall, he sipped his beer thoughtfully, "Burkett...Dobby said he played cards with Farkle. That big man must be Tiny Leatherwood. What's a deputy doin' playin' poker while on duty? Maybe he ain't on duty. That Mexican looks out of place in that game. Cowboy at th' back table is asleep...or drunk."

The only other people visible were two saloon girls who were sitting with a small, balding, fat man who had on a broadcloth suit. Morgan smiled, "Poor drummer. Those girls'll have him picked clean by nightfall."

The bartender brought a plate of food and placed it

nervously on the table. Morgan put a silver dollar next to the plate. When the bartender reached for it, Morgan grabbed his wrist. "Who might you be, friend?" he asked in a low voice.

"Phil Browne," he stuttered, definitely apprehensive.

Morgan squeezed his wrist. "Phil, I need some information."

Browne looked furtively toward the men at the poker table and then back to Morgan. "What kind of information?"

Morgan squeezed harder, "Th' poker players. Who are they?"

Browne hesitated and Morgan squeezed harder. "Ow!" he whined. "Th' one dealin' is Freeman Burkett. Th' Mex is Rafael Chacon..." His voice faded.

Morgan twisted Browne's wrist. "Phil, th' others."

Browne winced, "Th' big one is Tiny Leatherwood. Cowboy wearin' th' black shirt is Carl Zachary. Th' other one's Tom Gilkey."

Morgan released him and nodded to the man in the back.

Browne rubbed his wrist. "That's our town drunk, Joel Crow." Morgan shifted his gaze to the drummer and the saloon girls. Browne added, "Rita and Jodi...I don't recall th' drummer's name." Browne spun around and strode back to the bar.

Morgan let him get halfway there before he called out in a loud voice. "Thanks for th' information, Phil." His voice once again quieted the saloon. Morgan paused for a moment and added, "Keep th' change for your trouble."

Leatherwood gave Browne a hard look. Zachary threw his cards toward Browne and shouted, "Dammit to hell, Phil! Get some Goddamn drinks over here for Chris' sakes." He turned to Chacon, who was raking in the pot. "And I don't wanna hear any shit from you either, damn greaser. That's three hands in a row. If I didn't know better I'd—"

Leatherwood cut Zachary off, "You'd what, Carl?" He was staring at Morgan as he spoke.

"If he wins one more hand, I'm gonna—"

"Whine and spout off at the mouth," interrupted Leatherwood. "Damn, Carl, leave it lay."

The woman in red took a tray of drinks and a new deck of cards to the poker players. Morgan finished his beer and food and watched the poker game with added interest. Chacon kept winning as Zachary got louder and more agitated. Morgan was amused at how cool Chacon was and how indifferent Burkett, Leatherwood, and Gilkey seemed. The two saloon girls had left the drummer and were watching the poker game.

Morgan instinctively took the thong from the hammer of his pistol, thinking, "It's a set up. Any minute now…I wonder how they're gonna do it? Th' girls hafta be a part of it. This oughtta be interestin'." Zachary's loud voice focused Morgan's attention to the present.

"Mex, this is th' biggest pot of th' day, and I got your greasy ass this time." He slapped the table and hollered, "Rita, more drinks over here."

"I ain't deaf," answered Rita. She gave Zachary a cold stare before going to the bar for the tray of drinks that Browne had waiting for her.

"I raise ten dollars," said Chacon in broken English.

"Call and raise a hundred," smirked Zachary. Leatherwood, Burkett, and Gilkey threw their cards in. Zachary crowed, "Now it's just you and me, greaser."

Chacon studied his cards for a long time, and then placed them on the table. He stared at Zachary without speaking. "Call or fold, dammit," shouted Zachary.

"If you please, señor," said Chacon. "I'm thinking."

"With what?" chortled Zachary.

Chacon acted as though he hadn't heard the insult. He counted out a hundred dollars and placed it in the pot. "I call your bluff, Señor."

The saloon girl in red chose that moment to scream.

"Spider! Spider! There's a spider on me!" She began slapping at her dress and jumping up and down.

A wry smile creased Morgan's face as he watched and thought, "So that's their plan."

"Dammit t' hell, Rita," shouted Zachary. "We're tryin' to play poker here. There ain't no damn spider on you."

"You go to hell," she screamed. "He's down my front. I can feel him!" She was still dancing around, slapping and clawing at the front of her dress.

Leatherwood laughed, "Let him be, Rita. He's just wantin' to nurse a little. 'Sides, if he bites you, it'll serve him right."

"You go to hell, Tiny."

"No thank you," answered Leatherwood. "I've been there. I was married once."

Zachary spread his hand in front of Chacon and sneered, "Read 'em and weep, Mex. Two pair, kings over."

A faint smile appeared on Chacon's face. "Sorry, amigo. You lose again. Me, I have a straight." He turned his cards over; what he saw made his smile disappear.

After a moment, Zachary broke the unnatural silence. "A pair of deuces!"

"And that ain't all," said Leatherwood. "Th' greaser's got six cards."

Burkett casually added, "I guess Carl had him pegged all along."

"The cards, they are not mine," sputtered Chacon. "Someone…" His eyes were flashing as he stared at Rita and continued, "is trying to make me a fool, no?"

Zachary reached out to rake the pot. "Make you a fool? Not hardly." He raked the money to him and continued, "We're fixin' to make you what we make all cheatin' greasers."

"Yeah, dead," said Leatherwood.

Chacon sprang to his feet and backed slowly to the bar. His hand was poised near his gun, he spoke rapidly in Spanish then in English, "I did not cheat. The money, she is mine. I'll kill any man who says I cheated."

"He's right," said Morgan in a casual voice that quieted the saloon.

Leatherwood got up from the table and faced Morgan, who was now standing. "What'd you say?"

"I said he didn't cheat."

Leatherwood moved two steps away from the table. "Mister, you're stickin' your nose in a place it don't belong. One more word outta you, and I'm gonna break your back."

Morgan spoke to Chacon in Spanish, "Friend, watch the one in the black shirt." Chacon nodded his head in understanding. Morgan then said to Leatherwood, "You're gonna find th' easiest part of breakin' my back is tellin' me about it."

"Stranger, you'd better listen to Tiny," Zachary said. "He stomped a mud hole in th' last gent that crossed him."

"And then I walked it dry," chortled Leatherwood.

"Is that a fact?" Morgan's tone was casual. He slowly walked up to Leatherwood and added, "Th' money belongs to Chacon. Give it to him or make your play."

The words were barely out of Morgan's mouth when Leatherwood lunged forward and threw a vicious right hand. Morgan was expecting the big man's move. He moved quickly aside, at the same time landing a hard right hook that sent the unbalanced giant crashing into the bar. Morgan was on him quick as a cat. He kicked Leatherwood's feet out from under him, and, as he crashed heavily to the floor, Morgan drew his Colt and clubbed him over the head.

Morgan spun quickly around and found the other men with their hands up. Chacon had them covered. Morgan holstered his pistol. "Any one else want to try their hand at breakin' my back?"

"Mister, you're a dead man," said Zachary. "Nobody does that to Tiny. He's gonna kill you when—"

"You mean he can try," interrupted Morgan.

The sound of the bat-wings opening stopped all conversation. Sheriff Piper stepped in. Rideout followed. "What's the ruckus?" asked Piper calmly.

"This here stranger just pistol-whipped Tiny," answered Zachary.

Piper and Rideout walked over to the sprawled Leatherwood. "Ol' Tiny looks plumb peaceful," commented Rideout.

Piper turned to Morgan, "What's your story?"

Morgan shrugged, "Not much to tell." He looked at Leatherwood, who was groaning and showing signs of regaining consciousness. "He called it."

"That's a bunch of bullshit," spat Zachary. "We caught th' greaser cheatin', and he butted in."

"Looks like he did more'n butt in," commented Rideout. His voice was thick with sarcasm.

Piper turned to Burkett. "What about it, Freeman?"

"It's like Carl said." He nodded toward Chacon, "Th' Mex turned over six cards."

Piper looked at Gilkey, "Tom?"

"That's about th' size of it."

Piper thought for a moment, then shook his head in apparent amazement. "I see." He then asked Browne, "What've you got to add, Phil?"

Browne dropped the glass that he was wiping when Piper called his name. He picked up the glass with nervous hands and stammered, "I wuz workin' when all th' hell broke out."

"Uh-huh," said Piper. He then walked over to Chacon, who still had his pistol in his hand. "What's your side of it?"

Chacon holstered his pistol. "They lie, señor."

"He's not only a cheat; he's also a liar," said Zachary. "I won that money fair and square, Sheriff."

"We'll remember you said that," replied Morgan.

"You can't believe him either, Piper. He's just like th'

greaser. Hell, Sheriff, he spoke to the Mex in Spanish." He looked at the others and asked, "Didn't he?" All shook their heads "yes."

Piper held up his hand. "Enough! Looks to me like it's word against word."

"Not quite," Morgan replied.

Piper turned to Morgan, "How's that?"

Morgan stepped away from the bar. "I can prove Chacon didn't cheat." He walked over to Zachary and continued, "As a matter of fact, I can prove it was th' other way around."

"Are you callin' me a liar and a cheat?" snarled Zachary.

Morgan's eyes again were pitch black; he looked Zachary square in the eyes. "That's exactly what I'm sayin'." He walked back to the bar, leaned against it and said, "Leatherwood and th' little lady in red were in on it, too." Morgan looked at Burkett and Gilkey. "I'm not sure about th' other two."

Rita was trying to ease her way up the stairs when Piper stopped her. "Rita, get back down here." Her face turned blood red, but she flounced down the stairs and sat down noisily in a chair.

Piper turned back to Morgan, "Stranger, you've made some strong accusations. Suppose you show us your proof."

Morgan smiled, "Rita put on quite a show…hollerin' and such…carryin' on 'bout a spider. Most everybody in th' saloon was watchin' her." Morgan pushed his hat up on his forehead, paused for a moment, and continued, "Except th' drunk, th' one who switched th' cards, and me."

"That's an interestin' story," said Piper. "But it still ain't proof."

Morgan grinned, "How about if I tell you I saw it all happen, just like I said?"

"Still ain't proof," replied Piper. "It's still your word against theirs." A trace of irritation had crept into his voice.

"Damn right, it ain't proof," muttered Zachary.

"Shut your yap," snapped Piper. "You've had your say."

"I saw what I saw," Morgan said evenly. "Sheriff, give me a few minutes, and I'll clear up this whole thing to your satisfaction."

Piper sighed, "All right, but make it quick."

Morgan nodded his head, "Everyone return to where they were at th' time Miss Rita was puttin' on her act."

No one moved. Finally Piper said, "Oh, hell. Do what he says." Everyone complied, except Leatherwood.

Morgan pointed to his table, "I was sittin' back there; Phil was behind th' bar; Crow was where he is now; th' drummer was at th' table next to Crow. Jodi was standin' behind Gilkey, as I recall." Morgan paused for a moment as though deep in thought before he asked, "Am I right so far?"

"I suppose, but it still don't prove nuthin'," answered Burkett.

Morgan acted as though he hadn't heard Burkett. "Leatherwood was sittin' on Chacon's right; Zachary, here on his left. Rita brought a tray of drinks…" Morgan's voice faded away as he pointed to the tray on Chacon's right. After a moment he said to Chacon, "You said you had a straight and those cards (pointing to the cards in front of Chacon) weren't yours."

"Sí, señor. I swear on my mother's grave."

"Can you remember th' cards in your straight?" asked Morgan.

Chacon thought for a moment and replied in broken English. "Sí, Señor. The jack of clubs, the ten of clubs." He frowned and added, "The seven, eight and the nine. I think maybe they red."

Morgan returned to the bar and leaned casually against it. "Sheriff, I think you'll find somethin' of interest under that tray." He pointed to the tray on the poker table. He was watching Zachary as he did so. Zachary's face was ashen.

It was quiet as a cemetery at midnight in the saloon as Piper walked over to the table. He picked up the tray and said, "Well looka here." He turned over the cards he found there and called out, "Jack of clubs, ten of clubs, nine of diamonds, eight of hearts, seven of diamonds."

It was again deathly quiet for several seconds before Morgan broke the silence. "Leatherwood switched the cards."

Piper walked slowly back to the bar and announced, "Chacon, take your money and get on back to th' Circle H."

Chacon raked the money into his sombrero and walked slowly toward the door. As he passed Morgan, he said in Spanish, "Thanks, friend. I will not forget."

Morgan answered in Spanish, "Goodbye, friend. Watch your back from now on."

Piper was drumming his fingers on the bar. It was obvious he was about to make some hard decisions. "Rita, there's a stage through here tomorrow. Be on it." He pointed at Zachary, "And you! Get your ass out to th' Kiowa Lance." Zachary didn't move right away. His mouth was open, but no words came out. "Now!" said Piper. His voice cut like a knife.

Zachary was halfway to the door when Piper called after him, "And don't come back to Dog Bark 'til I send for you."

Piper stared at Burkett and Gilkey for several long moments before he said, "I'm half a mind to run you two birds out of town."

"Luther, I played no part in this," Burkett said evenly.

Piper stared at Gilkey, and Gilkey looked away. "I'll vouch for Tom," said Rideout. "Hell, Luther, Tom ain't smart enough…" Rideout didn't finish his sentence.

After a moment, Piper snapped, "Gilkey, get th' hell outta here." Gilkey grabbed his hat and sauntered out.

Leatherwood sat up and rubbed his head. "Son of a bitch. Who? What?"

Piper reached down and removed the deputy badge from Leatherwood's shirt. "Tiny, I've gone as far as I'm gonna with you. You're fired."

Leatherwood staggered to his feet, "I'm what? Who hit me? I'm gonna—"

Piper cut him off, "Rideout, help our ex-deputy over to th' sawbones." Rideout helped Leatherwood to a chair. Piper watched them for a moment and turned to Morgan, "You best be movin' on. Tiny ain't never been whipped before." He raised his eyebrows and added, "He holds a grudge somethin' powerful."

"I was plannin' on stayin' awhile."

Piper frowned, "Stayin'?"

Morgan nodded his head "yes" and handed Piper the letter of introduction from Marshall Reynolds.

Piper read the letter carefully. When he finished, he folded it and placed it in his shirt pocket and said, "Come see me after you get settled in th' hotel." He turned abruptly away, saying to Rideout, "Jack, kick Crow's drunk butt outta here. I told you a hundred times I don't want him layin' around drunk in here."

Morgan watched Piper, thinking, "That was easy. Maybe too easy."

Chapter Eight

Rideout finished telling Leatherwood what had happened, tossed Leatherwood a wet rag, and sighed, "Looks like you finally met your match."

Leatherwood wiped blood from his face and neck and turned to a smiling Rideout, "That'll be th' day. Th' son of a bitch caught me by surprise." He winced as he touched the cut in his scalp and asked, "Luther took my badge?"

"Yep," answered Rideout. "Hell, Tiny, he didn't have any choice. You and Zachary put him between a rock and a hard place with that dumb stunt you tried to pull on Chacon.

Leatherwood dabbed at the cut on his head. "What'd th' bastard hit me with?"

"Fist and gun barrel," offered Browne.

"Who in th' hell asked you, Phil," snarled Leatherwood. He pointed menacingly at the bartender and added, "When I'm through with him, you and me are gonna have a little talk about that conversation you and him had." He slung the rag toward Browne and whispered, "That damn pilgrim is gonna wish he'd never been born."

"I didn't tell him nothin', honest to God, Tiny," whined Browne.

"A pilgrim he ain't," deadpanned Rideout.

"I don't give a damn what he is," snapped Leatherwood. "He's gonna be six feet under come nightfall." He jerked out his pistol, checked the chambers, slammed it back into his holster, and asked, "Where'd th' bastard go to?"

Burkett was playing solitaire and didn't look up when he casually answered, "He's over at th' hotel."

Leatherwood walked gingerly to the bar, picked up his hat, and said, "He ain't gonna need no room, no sirree Bob. He's gonna learn what happens when you—"

Leatherwood was nearly to the door when Rideout stopped him. "What do you want on it?"

"What do I want on what?" shot back Leatherwood.

"Your grave marker." Rideout's tone was somber.

Tiny frowned, "Jack, I ain't in no mood for none of your damn jokes." He turned and stomped on to the door.

"Boys, ol' Tiny is fixin' to get himself killed by a gent named Stuart Morgan," announced Rideout.

Rideout's revelation quieted the room. Burkett put down his cards, and Browne dropped the bottle of whiskey he was holding. Leatherwood stopped in mid-stride; he slowly turned, took two halting steps back, and stammered, "Morgan?"

Rideout was smiling. "Yeah, Morgan."

Leatherwood stood statue-still for several seconds, looking at Rideout with unbelieving eyes. He finally walked back to Rideout, checked his pistol again, and said, "I don't care if it is him."

"You don't, huh?" chuckled Rideout.

Leatherwood sat down and smiled stiffly. "Hell no. I ain't afraid of him."

Rideout shook his head, "Then that makes you dumber'n dirt." His voice was friendly.

Browne whistled, "Stuart Morgan! In Dog Bark! I shoulda known it was him. He—"

Leatherwood cut him off. "Phil, I told you to shut up. Ain't gonna tell ya again." Browne ducked his head and began wiping the bar. Leatherwood turned back to Rideout and said smugly, "And I suppose you're not afraid of him?"

"No, I ain't," replied Rideout. "But I ain't no fool neither."

"Meaning I am."

"I didn't say that."

Burkett came over and joined them. "There's eight or ten men in Boot Hill who weren't afraid of him."

"Ya'll are beginnin' to scare me," quipped Leatherwood.

Rideout frowned, "Tiny, there's a big difference in bein' scared and bein' careful. Morgan's a man you gotta be careful with."

"Are you sure it's him?" asked Burkett.

"Yeah, I'm sure, and I'm sure of somethin' else, too."

"What's that?" Tiny asked.

"Farkle's mare came in yesterday, right?" Rideout paused, looked thoughtfully at the two men, and added, "And today his gun came in."

"His gun came in!" exclaimed Tiny. "What th' hell are you talkin' about?"

"I'm talkin' about keepin' your eyes open. A man would have to be blind not to notice that hawgleg of Farkle's."

"Get to th' damn point, Jack. For Chris'sakes," said Leatherwood.

Rideout grinned, "Morgan's packin' it. Might even be th' one he used to put that knot on your head."

Browne suppressed a chuckle, "Come to think of it, he did have a fancy iron stuck in his belt."

Leatherwood was fuming, "I'm gettin' pretty fed up with y'all's—"

Rideout interrupted and soothed, "No offense, Tiny."

Leatherwood studied Rideout for a moment and grumbled, "None taken."

Rideout scratched his chin, "What we need to ask ourselves is, how'd Morgan come by Ned's Colt? Farkle was better'n a fair hand with it."

"That's a good question," replied Burkett. "Ned prized that Colt. You can bet your bottom dollar he didn't give it up without a fight."

"You sayin' Morgan killed Ned?" Tiny questioned.

"I dunno," answered Rideout. "But I know one thing, if Morgan took it from him…" His voice faded away.

"It'd mean that Morgan—"

Rideout completed Burkett's sentence, "Is one dangerous hombre."

Silence enveloped the table for a moment. Tiny broke the silence. "Only man faster'n Ned in these parts is you, Jack." He paused for a moment and added, "Think you can take Morgan?"

Rideout, deep in thought, didn't answer right away. "Maybe. Maybe not, but if th' time comes, I'll pick th' place and time."

Burkett placed a freshly-rolled cigarette to his lips, "Word has it Morgan killed Frank Devlin last week."

"Th' gunman from Fort Smith!" exclaimed Leatherwood.

Rideout nodded his head "yes." "It's a fact. Piper told me." He grinned at Leatherwood, "You still want some of him?"

"Hell, yes. Like I said, I ain't afraid. There's more than one way to skin a cat." His words were emphatic, but his voice was less than convincing.

"First things first," said Rideout. "Let's find out what he's doin' here, and what that paper he gave Piper says." He grinned at Leatherwood, "Then we gotta figure out a way to get your badge back." Rideout got up from the table and added, "Meanwhile don't do nothin' foolish. Stay away from Morgan."

Tiny nodded his head grudgingly, "Okay, but I ain't afraid of him."

Rideout turned to Burkett, "Freeman, keep your ears open." He jerked Crow up by the collar of his shirt, "Time to go, Joel. Sheriff don't want no drunks in here."

Crow slurred, "I ain't botherin' nobody, dammit. I wuz jus'—"

"Wrong. Now, you're botherin' me." He shoved Crow toward the door. "Now get outta here before I lock you up."

After they had gone, Browne said to Burkett, "I'd sure like to be there when Morgan and Rideout tangle."

Burkett chortled, "Phil, you ain't even got th' guts to watch somethin' like that." He broke out in a full laugh, "Phil, Crow could whip your butt."

Morgan left the hotel, thinking, "Piper seems to be what Reynolds said he was. Rideout bears some watchin'. I'm probably gonna have to kill Leatherwood…sure ain't gonna turn my back on him. Haven't seen anyone fittin' Jubal's description; it's been a long time though. A man can change a lot in twenty years. Burkett's about his size and age. I'll have McEachern run a check on him."

Rideout was with Piper when Morgan entered the office. Piper studied Morgan for a moment before casually asking, "Why'd you leave Fort Worth?"

"Seemed like th' thing to do at th' time." Morgan returned Piper's stare, thinking, "Strange. I thought sure he'd ask about Reynolds."

Piper's next statement caught Morgan by surprise. "Th' job pays thirty a month." He tossed Morgan a badge and continued. "Plus an additional fifty cents for every arrest you make." Piper paused as though waiting for Morgan to speak. When Morgan only nodded his head, he continued, "Th' county's got an account over at th' general store. Ten dollars a month. Get what you need. You pay for your own cartridges."

He went to a map on the wall. "Come here and I'll show you th' layout." After Morgan joined him, Piper said, "Your main job is to keep th' lid on at Blackthorn and Hangin' Tree." He pointed first at Blackthorn which was located twelve miles to the north of Dog Bark, and then to Hanging Tree, which was located thirteen miles to the south.

Piper studied the map for a moment then said, "You'll notice that th' Kiowa Lance joins th' Circle H right here." He pointed to a spot slightly southeast of Dog Bark, and continued, "There's been some hard feelin's between th' two spreads of late. They get together now and then at that damn cantina and whorehouse in Hangin' Tree. All hell generally breaks loose when they do."

Piper returned to his desk, "Then you got th' riffraff spillin' outta Griffin, buttin' heads with Killpatrick's punchers in Blackthorn." Piper put his feet up on his desk and continued, "You can headquarter in either one. Take your pick; just don't spend all your time in one place." He paused, rubbed his hands together, and asked, "Any questions so far?"

Morgan was still studying the map when he answered, "Nope."

Piper studied Morgan then said, "Tiny couldn't follow orders. Spent most of his time here at Dog Bark." Piper drummed his fingers on the desk top for a moment before saying, "Morgan, I'm the law in Dog Bark County. If a man's gonna work for me, he's gotta understand that, and he's gotta follow orders. Tiny never could figure it out." Piper leaned back in his chair, stared at the ceiling for a spell, then asked, "You gonna have any problem with that?"

"Nope," Morgan answered evenly.

Piper put his feet down. "Good enough. You remember what I said, and we'll get along." He nodded to Rideout, who had been silent the entire time. "Rideout and me can handle things in Dog Bark. If you ever need help, get word to us; we'll come runnin'." Piper stood up and added, "Check in with me ever' two weeks or so. If I need you sooner, I'll send Rideout to fetch ya. All right?"

"I think I got it all," replied Morgan.

Piper grinned, "Good enough." Although Morgan hadn't asked any questions, Piper called after him as he turned to go, "Are you sure there's no more questions?"

Morgan had many questions in his mind, but he turned and said, "I can't think of any more."

"I got one," said Rideout. Morgan and Piper both looked at him. Rideout pointed to Farkle's Colt stuck in Morgan's belt. "Where'd you get that?"

Morgan's eyes found Rideout's. "He said his name was Ned Farkle." Morgan held his stare until Rideout broke his off, "Was he a friend of yours?"

Rideout's face was stiff. "Not hardly."

Piper laughed, "Now that's downright funny. Farkle and Jack—friends!" He tugged at his ear and added, "If I hadn't run Ned outta town—"

"I'd have killed him," interrupted Rideout curtly.

"How'd you come by it?" asked Piper.

Morgan placed Farkle's fancy six-gun on Piper's desk. "He had it in his mind to kill me. I felt otherwise." Morgan recounted his run-in with Farkle, but he left out the part about Farkle's gun being empty.

When Morgan was through, Piper asked Rideout, "Don't

make no sense. Who in Dog Bark would hire Ned?" He turned to Morgan, "Hell, for that matter, who here even knew you were headed this way?"

"I ain't got a clue," lied Morgan.

"Farkle'd gun his own mother if th' price was right," Rideout stated.

"Could be most anybody," said Piper. "Ned rode a wide circle. He worked at th' Kiowa Lance and th' Circle H for a spell and hung out with those cutthroats and thieves at Fort Griffin, Blackthorn, and Hangin' Tree."

Rideout picked up Farkle's Colt and rubbed it against his vest. "Whatcha aim on doin' with it?"

"I don't have any use for it," replied Morgan.

Rideout's eyes lit up. "Ned left owin' me sixty dollars, a poker debt..." His voice faded as he caressed the pistol.

"That's up to Morgan," commented Piper.

"Suit yourself. Like I said, I don't have any use for it."

After Morgan had gone, Piper said to Rideout, "Somethin' ain't right. I smell a rat."

Rideout punched shells into Farkle's Colt, twirled it deftly and deadpanned, "I knew a rat once. A cat ate him." He slid the Colt in his holster and said, "Meow!"

Chapter Nine

Morgan left Piper's office with a slew of new questions to ponder. He walked to the livery, thinking, "Why didn't he ask about his old friend, Reynolds, and why'd he hire me without checkin' first with Marshall Reynolds? Kinda strange, him not even swearin' me in. Unless I'm wrong, neither one of 'em seemed to know about Farkle tryin' to kill me. I don't think they even knew who I was at first. If he knew me, Rideout wouldn't have bothered askin' Willson and th' bootmaker. They never mentioned Bear Paw...or th' farmers. Piper didn't say a word about th' two deputies that were murdered...or th' missing deputy. It's strange, real strange."

Morgan entered the livery, still thinking, "That kills my

theory about Collins. Maybe he wasn't returning from Dog Bark, or maybe he did come to Dog Bark. Or maybe he met with someone else; or he was th' one who tried to bushwhack me. I wonder if—"

Willson's voice interrupted Morgan's thoughts. "I went ahead and put new shoes on all four. Back two needed it now, and it wuz just a matter of time on th' front ones."

"I'm obliged. What do I owe you?"

Willson noticed Morgan's deputy badge for the first time and smiled, "I didn't see th' badge when you came in today."

"Wasn't wearin' it." Willson's smile faded. Morgan asked again, "How much?"

"I usually get a dollar." Willson was still staring at Morgan's badge as he pocketed the dollar Morgan gave him, and asked, "You workin' for Luther?"

Morgan picked up Ebon's right back leg and nodded his head in approval. He dropped the horse's leg, turned to Willson and said, "Yes I am." He studied the frowning blacksmith for a moment and said, "That don't seem to sit too well with you. Care to tell me why?"

"It's not any skin off my nose," he muttered. "I've already said too much." He moved to the door muttering under his breath, "Anybody's better'n Leatherwood."

Before Morgan could reply, a young, towheaded boy burst into the livery. "Pa, he whupped Tiny and—" The sight of Morgan caused him to stop in mid-sentence. He froze, staring at Morgan with big eyes.

Willson scowled, "Tim, I've told you a hundred times to stay away from that saloon."

"I wasn't in th' saloon," replied Tim. "I was at th' general store…" The boy was still staring at Morgan and didn't finish what he was saying right away.

"Well, go on," said Willson.

"Sweepin' up 'cause Mister Crow wasn't able to. Mr.

Browne was tellin' everybody about th' fight." Tim's voice faded as he went over to Ebon's stall.

"Crow and Browne. Now there's a pair for you," Willson chortled. He turned to Morgan, "Tim's only ten. He thinks blowhards and bullies like Leatherwood and Browne hung th' moon." He shook his head and sighed, "And Crow...one of these days."

Morgan changed the subject. "Kyle, you wouldn't know anyone who'd like to earn two bits," he nodded to Tim, who was admiring Ebon, and continued, "brushin' Ebon, would you?"

"I'll do it, Pa! I'll do it!" Tim ran over to Morgan. "I'll be real careful, Mr. Morgan. I've brushed lotsa horses before." He went to Willson. "Haven't I, Pa?"

Morgan smiled, "It's all right with me if your pa—"

Willson waved his arm, "All right, all right." He ruffled Tim's hair and warned, "You be careful. That horse don't know you yet." He said to Morgan as Tim hurried back to Ebon, "Th' lad'll do a good job." He called to Tim, "Tim, when you're through, clean out them back stalls for your friend Crow. I'll be back in less'n an hour. I gotta fix that stove for your ma." He walked out muttering, "This is th' last straw. I've gone as far as I'm gonna.... Good fer nuthin' drunk."

Morgan watched Tim, who was standing on a wooden box in order to brush Ebon. Tim was saying, "Easy boy, easy. Feels good, don't it?"

Morgan walked to him, thinking, "Boy looks to have a natural way with horses. Ol' Ebon looks plumb happy."

Tim looked at Morgan, "You had him very long?"

"Since he was a colt," answered Morgan. "His name is Ebon."

"I'm savin' my money. Gonna get my own horse some-day." Tim stroked Ebon on the forehead, and said, "I bet you had your own horse when you were ten."

"More like twelve."

The two were quiet for a moment. Tim brushed Ebon as Morgan watched intently. Tim suddenly turned to Morgan. "Mr. Morgan, have you ever killed anybody?" His question caught Morgan off guard. He was trying to formulate an answer when Tim announced, "Deputy Rideout's killed fifteen men."

"Is that so? Did he tell you that?"

"Uh-huh and lots more," gushed Tim. "He lets me hold his six-shooter. He's got notches cut in…" He frowned as he realized what he'd said. "You won't tell my Pa, will you?"

Morgan smiled, "No, I reckon I won't. It'll be our little secret."

"Thanks. Pa'd whup th' tar outta me if he…can I see your gun?"

"No," said Morgan firmly.

Tim frowned, "Why not?"

"'Cause that'd make me th' same as Deputy Rideout."

Tim thought about that for a moment before saying, "I got a cat. His name is Gunsight. He's black and white, and I bring him scraps from Ma Weiss' kitchen."

"You shouldn't oughtta do that."

Tim had a puzzled look on his face. "Why not?"

"He can find his own food."

"But Ma Weiss is jus' gonna throw th' scraps away."

"That ain't th' point, Tim." Morgan found Tim's eyes and added, "You ain't doin' him no favor in th' long run. Cats are like people. You give 'em somethin' they don't work for, spoils 'em, and pretty soon they come to expect it. In th' long run we rob 'em of their pride and independence. Do you understand what I'm tryin' to say?"

Tim scratched his head, "But if he's hungry…and…and th' scraps are free—"

Morgan took the brush from Tim and began brushing

Ebon's mane. "Suppose you feed him for a year or two, and then somethin' happens to where you can't feed him anymore." Morgan gave the brush back to Tim, who was staring at him with a quizzical face, and added, "What's he gonna do then? After two years of bein' spoon fed, he's probably plumb forgot how to catch mice. Might even starve."

Morgan and Tim heard Crow as he stumbled into the livery. He eyed them with half closed eyes, and said with a thick tongue. "Whatcha starin' at? Ain'tcha never seen a sick man before?" He then lurched to the ladder that led to the loft, and after several attempts, managed to crawl to the top.

Tim watched Morgan stare after Crow. "My pa lets him sleep up there; he's suppose to clean out stalls and help Pa shoe horses." Tim pointed his brush toward the loft and added, "Pa says he's a drunk. Ma says he's got th' consumption."

Morgan watched and listened to Tim, but, at the same time, he was planning the day ahead. "Get up early tomorrow. See Witherspoon...go through back issues of th' newspaper. That oughtta provide some information. I'll get some provisions from th' general store and then mosey on down to Hangin' Tree..."

Tim broke Morgan's chain of thought. "Miss Farquar says Mr. Crow is shiftless and needs to be run outta town. Are you gonna run him outta town, Mr. Morgan?"

Morgan shook his head, gave the boy a quarter, and asked, "Who's Miss Farquar?"

Tim beamed, "She owns th' general store. She's purty." He bit the quarter before putting it in his pocket and stated, "Deputy Rideout tries to court her, but she won't talk to him."

"Is that a fact?" grinned Morgan.

"Yeah, and Mr. Browne says she's dead hand cold since her husband was killed." He frowned. "Tiny told Mr. Burkett she was colder'n a witch's tit." He paused for a moment, then asked, "Are you gonna court Miss Farquar?"

Morgan's grin widened, "No."

Tim thought for a moment, "Are you afraid of Deputy Rideout?"

Morgan's grin drooped, "No I ain't, Tim. Should I be?"

"I guess not," answered Tim. "But everybody else is... 'cept Sheriff Piper and me." He picked up a pitchfork and continued, "Thanks for lettin' me brush your horse, Mr. Morgan. I gotta clean them stalls out before Pa gets back."

He scampered to the back of the livery, leaving Morgan thinking, "I gotta be real careful with Rideout. When th' lead starts flyin', his'll be th' first and th' fastest."

Morgan returned to the hotel to clean up before going to supper. When he arrived at his room, he saw that the match he had leaned against the door had fallen. Morgan drew his gun, flattened himself to the wall, reached over, and gently tried the door knob. The door was locked. Morgan used his key, bent himself in half, and moved into the room quickly, with his Colt cocked and ready. Whoever had been there was gone.

Morgan holstered his gun and locked the door. "Someone was here all right. The Sharps and Winchester have been moved slightly. The saddlebags have been rifled. Someone wants to know more about me. Who?"

Morgan checked the rifles and his spare Colt and found them to be in working order. None of his other belongings were missing. He washed his face and hands, musing, "Whoever was in here was only lookin' for information, or they would've taken th' guns. That hotel clerk was mighty nervous when I checked in. I wonder?"

After Morgan had shaved and changed his shirt, he went downstairs to eat. On the way to the dining room he stopped by the desk to talk with the clerk. Bob Tucker put down his pen when Morgan came up. "Evenin' Mr. Morgan. Let me be th' first to welcome you to Dog Bark." He flashed a big smile and continued, "I said to myself when you checked in—"

Morgan cut him off. "Bob, a desk clerk in San Antonio once went through my belongings." Morgan's eyes had again become pitch black and hard, although his voice was casual.

The smile vanished from Tucker's face. "Why, Mr. Morgan, I never—" he stammered.

Morgan threw a small leather pouch on the desk. "I never said you did. I said a desk clerk in San Antonio did."

Tucker looked apprehensively at the pouch and whispered, "What's that?"

"Open it," ordered Morgan.

Tucker reached out with trembling hands and opened the pouch. When he saw what was in it, he dropped the pouch as though it was scalding his fingers and exclaimed, "What th' hell?"

Morgan picked up the pouch and emptied the contents on the desk. Tucker shrank back in fear and disgust as he stared at the two black, dried-up hunks of flesh. After several moments, Morgan put them back in the pouch and said dryly, "Bob, I got room for one more pair of ears in this pouch." Morgan locked onto the eyes of the frightened clerk, pocketed the pouch, and added, "I say what I mean, and I mean what I say."

Morgan was just finishing his meal when Tiny Leatherwood came in, his entrance immediately quieting the dining room. The big man walked directly to Morgan's table. All diners, except Morgan, had stopped eating and were anxiously awaiting the outcome of the meeting. Morgan continued eating, showing no outward sign that he was aware of Tiny's presence.

After several seconds of uneasy silence, Tiny whispered in a low voice that only he and Morgan could hear. "It ain't over twixt you an' me." Morgan put down his fork and looked up. Leatherwood smiled, "You didn't think that one little ruckus was th' end of it, did you?" He pointed at Morgan and added, "And that badge ain't gonna save your skin, neither."

Morgan stood up slowly, and softly said, "I never had no

such notion. I had a gut feelin' th' moment I laid eyes on you that I'd hav'ta kill ya someday. You're spoilin' my appetite. Now, make your play or git."

Tiny grinned, "Oh, I'm gonna make my play all right, but it'll be at my choosin'." He nodded to Morgan's gun, and continued, "And it ain't gonna be with these." He tapped his own gun, and added, "I aim to kill ya with my bare hands."

Morgan's eyes were black and hard, and his voice cold when he replied, "Like I said earlier, you're gonna find the easiest part is tellin' me about it."

Leatherwood leaned over and placed his hands on the table. "You're talkin' big now, gunfighter, but when I get my hands…" He lifted his hands and smiled wickedly as he admired them. "…'round your guzzler…" Leatherwood let his threat fade as he turned away, calling over his shoulder, "Somethin' else you oughtta know. I don't fight fair."

Morgan replied icily, "Neither do I."

Leatherwood sauntered to a table in the back, sat down heavily, and hollered, "Ma, burn me a steak. I'm hungry as a grizzly bear." He kicked an empty chair and sent it crashing into the wall, which, in turn, sent most of the diners scurrying toward the door.

Morgan was up early the next morning. He cleaned his firearms and went through his practice routine, right and left-handed. After eating breakfast, he went to the *Dog Bark Clarion.*

Myles Witherspoon, the editor of the Clarion, looked up from his desk when Morgan entered, and thought, "He whipped Tiny? And Piper hired him. It's sure peculiar him doing that." Witherspoon smiled when Morgan came up. "I'm Myles Witherspoon, Mr. Morgan. What can I do for you?"

Morgan returned his smile and stuck out his hand. "Stuart Morgan, Myles." As they shook hands, Morgan added, "You're th' first person in Dog Bark that don't seem put out by my bein' here."

Witherspoon thought, "He don't strike me as being like the others," as he said, "I suppose most are a bit jumpy all right, but after you've been here a while you'll…" He paused for a moment, ran his fingers through his gray hair, rethought what he was about to say, then asked, "What can I do for you?"

Morgan was thinking, "He wanted to tell me somethin' but thought better of it. He'll get around to it. I'd best not push him." Morgan pushed his hat back and replied, "If it ain't too much trouble, I'd like to go through your back issues."

Witherspoon raised his eyebrows. "All of them?" he was thinking, "What is he looking for?"

"If it's no trouble."

"Oh, it's no trouble," he answered. "It's just going to take awhile." He scratched his chin, and continued, "Let's see, first issue came out in, let me think…June '74. We do four issues per month, and this is May '80." He studied for a moment and frowned, "That's nearly three hundred issues." He looked balefully at Morgan and asked, "Are you sure you want to see all of them?"

Morgan nodded his head "yes" and smiled, "I'm a fast reader, and I got all day and tomorrow if I need it."

Witherspoon pointed to a table, "Have a seat. I'll bring them to you."

By noon Morgan had gone through over half of the issues. Checking his watch, he mused "I'm glad I thought of this. I would've had to ask a lot of questions; it's saved me a lot of time. Witherspoon's some newspaperman."

Morgan put his note pad in his shirt pocket and stepped over to Witherspoon, who was busily writing. "Myles, I'm gonna get a bite to eat. I'll be back in about an hour."

Witherspoon put down his pen. "I see you're making some progress." He smiled and asked, "Did you find what you're looking for?"

Morgan studied Witherspoon for a moment before casually replying, "Hard to say." He then brought up a question that made Witherspoon wince slightly. "I noticed two issues of June '79 are missing. What happened to them?"

Witherspoon smiled ruefully, "You've got a keen eye for detail. I didn't think you would notice." He sighed and continued, "Someone didn't care for my editorials concerning justice and law and order as practiced in Dog Bark so they wrecked my printing press and office."

"Is that a fact? Did th' sheriff find out who—"

Witherspoon tried unsuccessfully to suppress a laugh. "No, he didn't. He said it was probably just some drunk cowboys letting off steam." The two men said nothing for several moments, then Witherspoon added, "Speaking of the law, your friend Rideout came by twice. He appears to be quite interested in what you're doing in here."

Morgan held up three fingers. "Yeah, I saw him. What makes you think he's my friend?" His voice was casual, but his normally dark eyes had become like black agate.

"Oh, I don't know. I just assumed since you're both working for Piper..." Witherspoon's voice faded away.

"Things aren't always as they seem," replied Morgan. He subtly changed the subject. "I liked your weekly articles on new arrivals. Kinda catchy callin' it 'Dog Bark's Newest Barks.'"

Witherspoon reached for his nearby pen and pad. "I'm glad you mentioned that. I need some information on you. I'm sure our readers will want to know all about our newest arrival."

"Glad to oblige," grinned Morgan. "Full name is Stuart Lee Morgan, born 15 July 1848, San Antonio. Came here from Fort Worth. Deputy sheriff."

Witherspoon looked up, "Anything else?" There was a touch of disappointment in his tone.

"Nope. That about does it." A faint smile creased Morgan's

face as he added, "Your readers probably aren't interested in a simple man like myself."

Witherspoon watched Morgan leave, and thought. "Simple? Not hardly!" He returned to his desk, still thinking, "Myles, you'd better grease the printing press."

Chapter Ten

Morgan was just finishing his lunch when Rideout entered and approached him. "Sheriff wants to know when you're gonna start work."

Morgan put down his cup and eyed Rideout. "I've been on th' job since early mornin'." Morgan then continued with his lunch, paying Rideout no mind.

"I think he wants to know when you're movin' out to Hangin' Tree and Blackthorn," blurted Rideout.

"Tell Luther I'm goin' to Hangin' Tree in th' mornin'. I'll see him before I leave." Morgan took another bite of his steak, again ignoring Rideout's presence. After several moments of unnatural silence, an obviously irritated Rideout turned on his heel and strode out the door.

Morgan leisurely completed his meal, thinking, "I've got a feelin' they want me outta town. I wonder what they've got planned for me…on th' trail? Or maybe at Hangin' Tree or Blackthorn? A visit with Killpatrick and Haggard might turn up somethin'. I hope McEachern has some information for me. If Jubal Carver is here, he should make a move soon. I hope so."

Morgan's thoughts returned to what he'd discovered in the back issues of the *Clarion*. "Killpatrick was th' first to settle…spring of '67. Comanches drove him out in '68, but he returned in '72. Haggard came in '73…then th' first farmers in '74 and '75."

Morgan placed a coin on the table, "Town and county has really grown since th' last bands of Comanches and Kiowas went to Sill in '75."

Morgan's thoughts of Medicine Lodge Creek in 1867, and mused, "Hard to believe…less than ten years. Comanches and Kiowas all gone, except Bear Paw. Even Quanah…who would've thought? Damnation!"

When Morgan returned to the *Clarion*, he found Witherspoon conversing quietly with a middle-aged man who was dressed in a faded black suit. Morgan thought, "That's gotta be Doc O'Banion."

Morgan nodded to the two men and went to his table. In a few minutes Witherspoon brought O'Banion over. "Doc, I'd like for you to meet Stuart Morgan."

O'Banion held out his hand, "Doc O'Banion."

Morgan shook his outstretched hand, "Stuart Morgan, Doc."

Myles tells me I can expect an increase in business now that you're in town." His face and tone was stoic, but his eyes were active.

Morgan sensed immediately that he would take a liking to

O'Banion. He smiled, "You heard about my little scuffle with Leatherwood, huh?"

"Uh-huh. Me and everybody else in the county." He cut his eyes toward Witherspoon and winked, "We were sure sorry to hear ol' Leatherwood finally got his butt whipped."

Witherspoon went along, "Yep, pained us something awful, yes sir. Hated to hear it."

Morgan was thinking, "It's no secret how they feel." He picked up a paper and quietly said, "He didn't give me many options."

"You could have killed him," offered Witherspoon casually.

Morgan reflected on that and quietly said, "Yeah, I could've."

"You're probably gonna wish you had. I hear Tiny's threatened to kill you," commented O'Banion.

"Dog Bark's got a big ear," replied Morgan.

Witherspoon laughed, "The biggest." He became solemn, "Except when it comes to murder and robbery, bushwhacking, and such. Then nobody knows nothing, not even the law."

"Speaking of the devil," whispered Doc. "We've got company." He nodded toward the front window where Rideout was peering in. Witherspoon and O'Banion turned briefly toward the window. Morgan, who had already spotted Rideout, returned to his task.

After Rideout left, Witherspoon said, "Morgan, it's no secret that we've got trouble here in Dog Bark—big trouble." He looked at Morgan for several moments as though he wanted to continue, but was reluctant to do so.

Finally O'Banion said, "What th' hell. Morgan, we've been talking. Your coming here...standing up for Chacon... whipping Tiny. Then Piper still hires you." He paused, looked at Morgan, and frowned, "It don't make sense."

"I guess what we're asking is..." Witherspoon began.

O'Banion finished his sentence, "Whose side are you on?"

"What you really want to know is whether I'm here to solve problems or be a part of th' problem." Morgan accompanied the words with a friendly grin.

"Something like that," replied Witherspoon.

Morgan studied the two older men for a moment, and formed his answer carefully. "I agreed to come here as a favor to Marshall Reynolds of Fort Worth; he and Piper are old friends." Morgan paused, looked the two men square in the eyes, and lied. "Before I arrived here, all I knew about Dog Bark was what Marshall Reynolds told me."

"Which was?" asked Witherspoon.

"That Piper was having some problems, and, since I was heading this way anyway, he thought I might be of help."

O'Banion was frowning. "Piper asked for help?"

"Nope," answered Morgan. "Marshall Reynolds said it wasn't his style. He gave me a letter of introduction, which I gave to Piper."

Witherspoon and O'Banion looked at each other with obvious skepticism. Morgan continued, "Just now you asked whose side I was on?" Witherspoon and O'Banion nodded their heads, and Morgan continued, "I'm on th' side of law and order." His expression and tone of voice left no doubt as to the sincerity of his words.

"Good enough," said O'Banion, pointing to the newspapers in front of Morgan and adding, "You'll find it in there, but I'll warn you anyway." With one eyebrow raised he continued in a concerned voice, "The last three deputies who were for law and order are either dead or have disappeared."

"Is that a fact?"

"It's a cold, hard fact," replied Witherspoon. "I'd watch my back if I were you."

A wry smile creased Morgan's face as once again his eyes became hard and black. "I aim to."

The three men were quiet for a while, immersed in their

own thoughts. O'Banion broke the silence. "Dog Bark's a powder keg, Morgan. Myles wants to bet me five dollars you're the spark that's going to set it off."

Morgan put down the paper he was holding, looked into the distance for several seconds, then calmly said, "Time will tell. I'll cross that bridge when I come to it." He gestured for the two men to come closer, and after they complied, he whispered, "You'll be th' first to know, if and when I decide to light th' fuse."

O'Banion said to Witherspoon as they left Morgan, "Five dollars, huh? No bet."

Morgan went through the remaining issues of the paper in just over two hours. As he completed the final issue, he put his note pad in his shirt pocket, thinking, "Very interesting. Things are startin' to make a little more sense, maybe."

Morgan's next stop was Farquar's General Store. He saw her standing behind the counter and thought, "Tim was right. She is pretty, uncommonly pretty." Morgan walked to her and placed his list of supplies on the counter.

Linda Farquar picked up the list and asked, "Personal or county?" Morgan noticed the slight frown on her face and sensed a touch of contempt in her voice.

"County."

She studied his list for a moment, then looked him up and down before saying coolly, "No bullets?"

"Nope. Got plenty," replied Morgan evenly. He found her eyes and gazed into them until she looked away.

She turned, took several steps, then turned back and said bluntly, "Don't bother asking. I don't want to go for a buggy ride. I don't want to go on a picnic. I don't dance with…" She paused and continued tersely, "In short, Mr. Morgan, I don't socialize with gunmen."

"Pretty women all have th' same problem," replied Morgan evenly.

His reply surprised her and caused a slight flush to spread across her face. All she could manage to say was "Problem?"

"Yes Ma'am, problem." Morgan let a wry smile appear on his lips. "They assume every man wants 'em."

"Why I never…" Her voice died as she struggled with her thoughts. Her face flamed, then turned ashen. She stared blankly at Morgan for a moment before blurting out, "And I suppose you—"

Morgan interrupted, "No Ma'am, I don't." He let her think on that for a moment and added, "And you're wrong on another account also. I'm not a gunman. I'm a lawman. There's a difference."

Linda regained some of her composure and asked, mockingly, "What are Rideout and Piper…and that bully, Leatherwood?"

"I wouldn't know. I ain't wearin' their boots."

She studied on his last statement for a moment before saying coolly, "I'll fill your order." She turned stiffly and began to gather his provisions.

Morgan surveyed the store, thinking, "She's carryin' a lot of hate. Store's clean, neat…carries a woman's touch." He noticed an Indian lance and two arrows mounted on the wall over the door, and thought, "They're out of place. Not in character with the rest of th' store."

Morgan pointed to the lance and arrows, "I see you're interested in Indian weapons."

Linda put a small sack of coffee on the counter, "Interested! For your information, Mr. Morgan, those red heathen implements were used to kill my husband and father." She paused as though waiting for his reply, and when she saw that one wasn't immediately forthcoming, she added bitterly, "I have them up there to remind me of how much I hate the Comanches."

"Hate's a heavy burden to carry."

Linda frowned, "You don't hate the Comanches?"

Morgan stepped to the door, pointed at the two arrows, "No, I don't; nor th' Kiowas either."

Her frown deepened, "Kiowas?"

"Th' two arrows are Kiowa."

"But, it was the Comanche that…the army said—"

"Th' Comanche and th' Kiowa were friends; often hunted and raided together."

His revelation about the Kiowas caused Linda some confusion. "You mean hunted and butchered, don't you?"

Morgan sighed, "Ma'am, I'm sorry about your husband and father, but I'm not gonna argue about who's right or who's to blame." He saw she was looking at him as though seeing him for the first time. Morgan instinctively knew what she was thinking. He smiled sardonically and said matter-of-factly, "My grandmother was quarter Comanche, my mother was Mexican."

Linda blushed as she realized he'd known what she was thinking. She was momentarily stunned, but finally managed to quietly say, "Still, you know how they are—what they do…" Her voice trailed away.

"Yeah I do. From first-hand knowledge."

"And you still don't hate them!" Before Morgan could reply, she added, "It's because you're part…?" Once again her voice faded.

"Breed is th' more common word," said Morgan calmly. His eyes turned a shade darker as he continued, "No, I don't hate 'em. Hatin' th' Comanche and Kiowa don't make any sense, no matter who or what you are."

She stared at Morgan in complete amazement. "Don't make sense? After all the things they've done."

Morgan studied for a moment before saying, "It'd be like hatin' th' sun 'cause sometimes it's too hot."

Morgan's last statement jumbled Linda's thoughts; all she

could do was stand and stare. Morgan busied himself with his provisions she had assembled. She eventually said placidly, "I can see you're an authority on several subjects. And you're a philosopher and a detective, too."

Morgan smiled, "Your words, not mine."

"Let's see…women and Indians." She raised her eyebrows, looked discerningly at Morgan and continued, "Oh, yes, we mustn't forget cats and ears."

Morgan placed his provisions in the box which she had provided and quietly said, "I see you've been talkin' to Tim and th' hotel clerk."

She put her hands on her hips, "Scaring that boy. Telling him his cat is going to starve, and he shouldn't feed him, shouldn't let him become—dependent." She paused for a moment and then sputtered, "What if people didn't have to depend on each other?"

"Yeah, what if," replied Morgan. He picked up the box of provisions and added, "Like I said before, I didn't come here to argue." Morgan touched the brim of his hat, "Good evenin', Miss Farquar."

Morgan was near the door when Linda said, "Mr. Morgan, I'm not sure I like you."

Morgan turned and said, "All right."

"All right!"

Morgan smiled faintly, "What'd you expect me to say?"

She ignored his question, "You truly don't care if I don't like you?" Her tone was skeptical.

"Miss Farquar, I learned some time ago that I couldn't control what people thought about me. It's been a comfort to me ever since, just knowin' that."

Linda's lips were tight, "You are the most arrogant, opinionated man I've ever met."

"It's been said of me before, but like I said, your words, not mine." His smile widened, and his eyes flashed as he added,

"You said you weren't sure whether you liked me. That leads me to believe you haven't made your mind up yet." He returned to the counter, put the box down, and continued, "I'm reminded of a mare I once owned. I didn't like nothin' 'bout that filly th' first two months or so. I even threatened to sell her or turn her loose, anything to get shut of her."

Morgan picked up his provisions, snapped his fingers, "Just like that she came around. She turned into one of th' best horses I'd ever had. I loved that horse...wouldn't part with her for th' world." He moved toward the door.

Linda called after him, "And?"

Morgan sighed, "She stepped in a prairie dog hole one dark night and broke her leg." He opened the door, turned, and added, "I had to shoot her."

Linda stared at the door for several moments, thinking, "He's laughing his head off...at me." The thought infuriated her.

Chapter Eleven

Morgan left Dog Bark in the dead of night. He walked
Ebon quietly for ten minutes or so toward Hanging Tree
before circling back and taking the trail to Blackthorn. His
desire to depart unnoticed went as planned. The only person
he saw was Joel Crow, but Morgan was pretty sure Crow
didn't see him; Crow was face down on the livery floor,
snoring.

Morgan was halfway to Blackthorn when the crimson rim
of the sun peeked over the horizon. Morgan had kept Ebon at
a steady lope as he allowed his thoughts free reign, "Goin' to
Blackthorn instead of Hangin' Tree ought to buy me a couple
of days. I'll spend most of today gettin' th' feel of

Blackthorn…then I'll go on to Fort Griffin tomorrow…see what McEachern has dug up. Maybe I'll run into Coldiron—"

Morgan guided Ebon off the trail into a grove of red oak and live oak trees where he climbed down and took a pull from his canteen. "I'll rest for a minute. I might not be as smart as I think."

When ten minutes had passed, and Morgan hadn't heard or seen anything to arouse his suspicions, he mounted Ebon and continued to Blackthorn. His thoughts turned to what he'd read in the back issues of the *Dog Bark Clarion*. "Witherspoon wrote that one of th' deputies had been killed by an Indian renegade…caught an arrow in th' back as he was returning to Dog Bark from Blackthorn. Th' other one had been shot in th' back in Hangin' Tree. Gonna talk to O'Banion and th' undertaker. Maybe they know somethin' they don't know they know."

Morgan rode into Blackthorn, "Not much of a town," he said to Ebon as he rode slowly down the dusty main street. "Except for th' name, this could be any one of a hundred towns I've been in. One day people are here…next day they're gone…takin' their memories and disappointments with 'em… leavin' behind shattered dreams, a few weathered boards…and their dead."

Morgan stopped in front of Blackthorn's only saloon, the Black Deuce. He tied Ebon to the rail as he surveyed the almost vacant street, taking note of the two horses at the adjoining rail. He entered the Black Deuce thinking, "Those horses have been rode hard and recent…probably cowhands from th' Kiowa Lance. Dobby said Farkle often played poker in here with Burkett and Zachary. Maybe someone'll remember somethin'."

Morgan stopped just inside the saloon to let his eyes adjust to the darkness. He removed the thong from the hammer of his

Colt as he studied the interior carefully. It was typical of most small frontier saloons. There were four tables with four straight chairs around each. The bar was made up of four flour barrels and two planks.

Only two people were visible to Morgan; the bartender and a red-headed cowboy, who was sitting at one of the tables. Morgan moved to the bar, but he kept his eyes on the man at the table.

The bartender, a bald, fat man, took the cigar from the corner of his mouth and said, "You th' new law from Dog Bark?"

"That's right," replied Morgan still watching the man at the table, "Two horses...one cowboy...two glasses...Th' other one's here, but where?"

"Word has it you whipped Leatherwood's ass." The fat man's voice was flat.

Morgan neither confirmed nor denied the bartender's statement; instead he said loud enough for the man at the table to hear, "I'm Stuart Morgan, deputy sheriff out of Dog Bark."

"Coy Treywick, Morgan," said the bartender. The man at the table gave no indication that he had heard, but Morgan knew that he had. Treywick continued, "It's about time Piper—"

"Sheep dip," interrupted the cowboy. "That ain't your name."

"What'd you say?" asked Treywick. His voice had an edge to it.

"Mind your own business, fat man. I ain't talkin' to you."

Morgan moved away from the bar. "Then you must be talkin' to me."

"Well, now, ain't you th' one?" The cowboy moved away from the table and added, "Who else would I be talkin' to?" He looked around the dark room, "Ain't nobody else here but me, you, and th' tub of guts."

Morgan glanced at Treywick and saw that he was rubbing his brow with two fingers. Morgan moved a step farther away from Treywick and the bar and announced, "If your friend doesn't show himself in five seconds, I'm gonna kill ya where you stand." Morgan's black eyes bored holes in the stranger. The tone of his voice left little doubt of his sincerity.

Morgan saw the first flicker of fear and apprehension creep into the stranger's eyes, and it confirmed what he already knew; there were two of them. The stranger laughed nervously, showing a mouth full of bad teeth, "Friend, you've been out in th' sun—"

Morgan cut him off, "You're down to two seconds." The stranger's eyes got bigger; he stood as though mesmerized. "Times up," Morgan said quietly.

The cowboy finally found his tongue; he raised his hands and stammered, "Come on out, Catfish." After a moment of strained silence, a door in the back of the room opened quietly, and a tall, thin man with a pronounced lantern jaw stepped quietly into the saloon.

Catfish walked jauntily to the end of the bar and chuckled, "Jim Bob, looks like we got us a live one."

Jim Bob had regained most of his composure and all of his smile. He leisurely removed a pair of thin leather gloves from his gun belt, slipped them on his hands, and replied, "But not for long." He paused, nodded toward Catfish, and said to Morgan, "You still think you can kill me?"

"Yep," replied Morgan. Then he stunned both men with a lightning quick draw. His Colt was pointed at Jim Bob, who had barely managed to get his pistol halfway out of its holster; Jim Bob froze instantly as he stared unbelieving at Morgan. Catfish hadn't even managed to get his hand on his gun, so he slowly raised both hands. Morgan stared at Jim Bob and whispered, "Any time I want to;" his Colt bellowed twice.

Morgan's first shot shattered Jim Bob's hand and ricocheted of the walnut grip of his six-shooter; his second shot gouged splinters inches from the plank in front of Catfish.

Jim Bob dropped to one knee, holding his right wrist with his left hand. He looked at Morgan with eyes filled with pain and shock and cursed, "Goddamn! Son of a bitch! My hand! You've shot my hand off!"

Morgan paid him no mind as he said to Catfish, "Two fingers—put it on th' bar." Catfish knew what he meant; he slowly pulled his pistol and placed it on the bar.

"Now move away," ordered Morgan.

Catfish moved back, whining, "Damn, mister…you had no call to do that. We thought you were somebody else."

"Well, you thought wrong," interrupted Morgan. "Maybe you'll be more careful next time." He turned to Jim Bob, "Get over here." Jim Bob got to his feet and staggered over to Morgan. His hand was a bloody mess. "Turn around," ordered Morgan. After the wounded man complied, Morgan took the pistol from his holster then put his foot on Jim Bob's butt, and shoved him violently toward Catfish.

Morgan walked calmly to the end of the bar where he methodically unloaded the two men's six-shooters, each cartridge punctuating the heavy silence as it hit the floor. Morgan cocked the first pistol, took it by the barrel, and slammed it against the bar, knocking off the hammer. Then he took the other pistol and repeated his action. Morgan walked slowly to the two shaking men and shoved the busted six-shooters into their holsters.

Morgan returned to the bar and asked Treywick, "How much do they owe you?"

Treywick was sweating profusely; he wiped his brow with a trembling hand and said in a shaky voice, "Let's see…they had three drinks…That'll be—"

"Twenty dollars," said Morgan, to which Treywick smiled.

"Twenty dollars!" cried Catfish. "We ain't gonna pay—"

"Give 'em th' fuckin' twenty dollars," spat Jim Bob. "For Christ sake...I gotta get to a doctor...I'm bleedin' to death." He lurched toward the door, saying, "There'll be another day."

Catfish moved to the bar and gave Treywick a twenty-dollar gold piece. "Whole damn place ain't worth twenty dollars."

Morgan stopped them at the door. "If I see you again in Dog Bark County, it'll be self defense as far as I'm concerned." Morgan went to the door and watched them ride off. He returned to Treywick and said, "Let me see th' gold piece." Treywick fished it from his vest pocket and handed it to Morgan. Morgan saw that it was a 1878 S double eagle. He gave it back to Treywick, thinking, "1878 S...same as th' ones Farkle was carryin'."

Morgan took a seat at one of the tables with his back to the wall, where he could see both entrances. He took out his note pad and leafed through it until he found what he was looking for. "Army payroll...robbed...over ten thousand in gold taken." Morgan returned the pad to his shirt pocket and thought, "That was in January. Coldiron will know th' dates and mint marks...just could be."

Treywick came over and sat down uninvited. He pushed a glass of beer toward Morgan. "It's about time Piper sent us someone. Leatherwood was worthless as tits on a boar hog. Never was here when we needed him. When he was here, all he did was guzzle beer, on th' cuff. He still owes me eight dollars. I'll say this, though, When Walsh was deputy things got takin' care of. It's a shame somebody killed him."

Morgan hadn't been paying much attention to Treywick until he mentioned Walsh. "You said killed? What makes you think he was killed?"

"Oh I know they've never found his body." Treywick leaned over, raised his eyebrows, and continued, "But he's sure enough dead all right." Then he lowered his eyebrows and his voice, "Just like them other two."

Morgan took a sip of beer and asked, "When was th' last time Walsh was here?"

Treywick frowned, "Let's see. Damn, it's been awhile." He scratched his huge stomach. "About five months ago. Yeah, now I remember. It was a Friday night…rainin' buckets. To my knowledge, that's the last anyone ever saw him."

Morgan thought for a moment. "Do you remember who else was here that night?"

"Same bunch as always," laughed Treywick. "They were regular as clockwork in those days, every Friday night. Let's see…Burkett, Zachary, Farkle, and Smith, and Collins, and sometimes Leatherwood."

"Who's Smith?"

"Toby Smith. He and Carl Zachary are punchers out at the Kiowa Lance."

"And Collins?"

"Deputy from Fort Griffin."

"What time did Walsh leave?"

Treywick pondered the question for a moment and said, "As best as I can recollect, he left just before daybreak."

"What about th' poker players? Anyone leave before or shortly after Walsh?"

"Nope. I remember clearly. That game didn't break up 'til nine or so."

Morgan thought for a while and asked, "What time did Walsh come in that night?"

Treywick frowned, "Funny you should ask that. I'd almost forgotten. I thought it was strange at th' time. He came in th' back door 'round two."

"Did Walsh talk to any of th' poker players?"

"Not that I remember, except for th' usual howdies."

Morgan studied on what the fat man had told him, then asked, "What about th' other deputy?"

Treywick shook his head, "That was over a year ago, but

as best as I can recollect…" His voice faded as he thought back. "You know, come to think of it, it was a Friday night also. I remember now. Same bunch was playin' poker… no…no, it wasn't th' same bunch. Leatherwood wasn't here, but, now I remember, that drunk from Dog Bark was here, passed out. I locked him in here when I closed up."

Morgan put a nickel on the table. "Thanks. I'll be around."

"I hear Ned Farkle is dead," Treywick deadpanned.

"You heard right."

"I also heard it was you who killed him."

Morgan returned to the table. "Who'd you hear it from?"

"Collins came through here several days ago tellin' about it. Why do you ask?"

"Just curious, that's all." Morgan reloaded his Colt and asked Treywick, "Have you ever seen those two birds before?"

"Nope. I never before laid eyes on 'em."

"When did they come in?"

"'Bout an hour before you showed."

"Did they say anything?"

"Naw, real quiet, they wuz."

Morgan moved outside. Treywick followed. As Morgan was surveying the mostly vacant buildings and street, Treywick asked, "Piper got you bouncin' betwixt here and Hangin' Tree?" Morgan nodded his head, to which Treywick smirked, "You're gonna find that Blackthorn's Kansas City compared to Hangin' Tree."

"Is that a fact?" replied Morgan. He climbed on Ebon and rode slowly toward Dog Bark.

Treywick called after Morgan, "Tell Tiny I want my damn money."

Morgan rode on, thinking, "Yeah, I'll tell him." Morgan didn't know exactly what he was looking for, but he knew he'd know as soon as he spotted it. He rode slowly, scanning both sides of the trail, thinking, "I have a hunch Walsh was killed soon after he left Blackthorn…th' killer probably picked a high spot to shoot from, down to a spot on th' trail where it was free of trees and brush."

Morgan rode on, looking for such a place. His thoughts returned to what Treywick had told him. "Leatherwood, Zachary, Burkett, Smith, and Collins were there…didn't leave. That leaves Piper and Rideout unaccounted for." Morgan was a disciplined thinker. He knew from experience that the obvious wasn't always obvious.

He went over all that Treywick had said and thought, "What about Treywick? Why should I believe him? Where was he at th' time Walsh was killed?" Morgan rubbed Ebon's neck and mused, "Ebon, only th' poker players can answer those questions. Maybe I'll just have to ask 'em."

Morgan's thoughts returned to the business at hand when he spotted a place that fit what he was looking for. A feeling of both excitement and apprehension passed through his body as he slid off Ebon and gazed up to an elevated spot to his left. "Perfect spot for it. Only sixty yards or so, rocks and brush for cover…Rider would be facin' th' bushwhacker. He'd have a clear shot."

Morgan climbed to the spot and searched for anything that might prove his theory. He searched in vain for nearly ten minutes, and was about to give up when he saw it. Morgan bent down and extracted a shell casing from a crack in one of the two boulders. He knew immediately what it was. "Sharps," he said aloud.

Morgan searched for another minute or so and found nothing else of interest. He put the Sharps cartridge casing in his pocket and thought, "Might not mean a thing, but it might." Morgan still had the feeling that he was on to something and he said to himself, "If I was to shoot someone from here, and wanted to get rid of th' body before someone happened along…what would I do? I wouldn't drag th' body up here…it'd be too hard…take too long."

He looked down at the trail and thought, "Th' terrain slopes considerably to th' right of th' trail. Easiest and fastest way would be to roll him or drag him down into that gully. Yes sir, that's what I'd do. I'm bettin' that's what he did."

Morgan came around a bend in the dry creek bed and found an old weathered boot. He picked it up and thought, "I was right. I can feel it in my bones. I'm guessin' he's in a shallow grave and not far from here." Morgan noted that the boot showed signs of an animal having chewed on it, and thought, "Probably coyotes or wolves."

Morgan moved another twenty yards or so down the dry creek bed and found what he somehow knew would be there. As he moved closer to the clump of brush and rocks, he saw what was left of a human foot protruding from under the brush and rocks.

Chapter Twelve

Morgan hunkered down by the grave and thought, "He could've heard somethin' that night...or they might have thought he heard somethin'." Morgan began to remove brush and rocks. "It's possible no one at th' game killed him. Maybe someone else knew where he'd be and waited for him...another possibility...someone found out he was a U.S. Marshall."

Morgan pulled the last of the rocks and brush from the grave and mused, "Either way, his luck ran out." Although the body was badly decomposed, Morgan knew he was looking at Chris Walsh; his deputy badge was still pinned to his vest. Morgan had seen death many times before, but somehow seeing Walsh and thinking about the wolves and coyotes tearing at his body caused Morgan to experience a feeling like none he had ever felt before. He stood there for a long time, staring at the mangled, decomposed corpse and thinking.

After a while Morgan did what he had to do; he examined Walsh's body. He found nothing in his pockets and thought, "Th' killer removed every thing...he left his six-shooter though." Morgan then checked Walsh's body more closely. "It was a Sharps all right...big hole...broke his spine. Shot him between th' eyes, too...six-gun. Killer wasn't takin' any chances."

Morgan recovered Walsh's body, adding more rocks so that the coyotes and wolves couldn't get at him again. He placed the last rock on the grave and said, "Best I can do for you now, but I'll make you a promise. I ain't gonna rest 'til whoever did this..." Morgan's voice died away before he finished his thought aloud.

Morgan rode wide around Blackthorn and pushed on to Fort Griffin, stopping often to watch and listen. He was very much aware that whoever had killed Walsh and the other two deputies probably had the same fate planned for him. The trip to Fort Griffin was uneventful, and Morgan rode Ebon into the livery just as the sun slid under the horizon.

Asa Whitmore walked up as Morgan climbed down. "Fort Worth, right?"

Morgan handed him the reins and grinned, "I figured you'd sniff it out eventually."

Whitmore chuckled, "Hell, you ain't no secret anymore. Everybody in town's talkin' 'bout you...gunnin' Farkle, an' kickin' Tiny Leatherwood's butt." He pointed to Morgan's badge. "That cost me a dollar."

"How's that?"

"I bet Dobby that Piper wouldn't hire you."

Morgan smiled and shrugged his shoulders, "Well, knowin' you, you've figured some way to get it back."

Asa grinned, "You're right as rain. I bet him two dollars this mornin' that you'd run Jim Bob and Catfish outta Blackthorn by tomorrow."

Morgan's smile vanished. "What can you tell me about 'em?"

"Not much really. Dobby ran 'em outta here yestidy. When they come for their hosses, they told me they wuz goin' to Blackthorn."

"Have you seen 'em since?"

"Shore 'nuff have. They came howlin' in here 'bout two hours ago, cussin' and carryin' on 'bout you shootin' Jim Bob's hand off."

Morgan thought for a moment and asked, "Are they still here?"

Whitmore laughed, "Naw. Dobby sent 'em packin' after Doc fixed up Jim Bob's hand."

"Which way did they go?"

Whitmore pointed North. "Mad as hell, they wuz. Jim Bob swore he'd kill ya th' next time he saw you."

Morgan thought, "Not on his best day." He handed Whitmore a dollar. "Room and board for th' both of us." He started out, then turned and asked, "Is Collins around?"

Whitmore scratched his chin, "I'm not sure. I ain't seen him since early mornin'."

"Thanks, Asa." Morgan walked to Wasserman's lunch room, thinking, "That was McEachern's horse at th' livery. More'n likely he's at th' lunchroom, th' saloon, or th' hotel."

Morgan entered the lunchroom and saw McEachern sitting at a table with two cowboys. He went to their table and said, "It's a mite crowded tonight. Mind if I join you?"

The two cowboys looked at Morgan uneasily but nodded their heads "yes." "Not at all," replied McEachern. "Have a seat." After Morgan sat down, he added, "I'm Will Taylor, cattle buyer. I just got into town."

"Stuart Morgan," said Morgan. "I'll have th' stew an' cornbread with a glass of milk," he said to a woman who had approached his table.

After the woman left, McEachern asked Morgan, "Are you th' local law?"

"Nope. Dog Bark."

"Dog Bark? Then maybe you can tell me about th' Kiowa Lance. I hear they've always got cattle for sale."

Morgan took the plate from the woman and nodded to the two cowboys, "These gents probably know more 'bout that than me. I'm new in Dog Bark."

One of the cowboys said through a full mouth, "Old man Killpatrick's always got cattle for sale." He swallowed hard and added, "But you'd better know your business."

The other cowboy smiled, "He'd skin his mother for a dollar."

"If you got th' time," said the first cowboy, "You'd do better in th' long run to deal with Haggard down at th' Circle H."

Morgan ate in silence as McEachern and the two cowboys continued their conversation. After the cowboys were gone, Morgan said softly as he looked at his plate, "One hour...I'll be at th' livery." McEachern gave no indication that Morgan had spoken to him. He placed a coin on the table and left.

Morgan waited for five minutes before he left the lunch-room. He walked to Dobby's office, thinking, "Maybe Dobby can shed some light on Jim Bob and Catfish. I wonder if I should tell him about Collins?" Morgan pushed open the door and thought, "No, I reckon not."

Tom Dobby smiled as he recognized Morgan. "Good to see you again. I see you're totin' tin again."

Morgan shook his outstretched hand, "Hello, Tom." Morgan pushed his hat up and sighed, "You know how it is. I suppose it gets in your blood."

"Yeah, I do. What brings you back to Fort Griffin?"

Morgan lied, "I ran two yahoos outta Blackthorn this mornin'. I kinda figured they might head this away."

Dobby frowned, "You figured right. They came in two, three hours ago." He grinned and added, "Th' red-head's gonna be left-handed for a while."

"Tom, they meant to kill me. Have you heard anything?"

Dobby shook his head, "Not a word, Stuart. All I can tell you is they drifted in here th' day after you left—said they were from Oklahoma City. I ran 'em outta town th' same day, just like I did today when they came back."

Morgan thought for a moment. "Tom, if you see 'em again, let me know."

"I'll do it. Now let me buy you a drink, and you can fill me in on what's goin' on down at Dog Bark."

"All right, but I'm buyin'."

"You talked me into it," Dobby grinned.

The two lawmen ended up having two beers and a lot of conversation. Morgan lost track of time, but he came away with the feeling that Dobby could be counted on if the need ever arose. He entered the livery, thinking, "Maybe McEachern is still here—"

McEachern's voice floated quietly down from the loft, "Stuart, up here." Morgan climbed quickly to the loft. The two men shook hands. "I was hoping you'd show up today. How're things at Dog Bark?"

"Have a seat. It's gonna take awhile." Morgan brought McEachern up to date on all that had happened since they had last talked. He held back on finding Walsh until the last. "Wallace, I've got bad news."

"How bad?"

"Th' worst."

"Walsh?"

"Uh-huh. I found him this mornin'…in a shallow grave

outside of Blackthorn."

McEachern didn't speak for a while. Morgan waited for McEachern to gather himself. He finally said, "I think it's best we leave him where he is." His voice cracked, and he struggled to continue, "'til this is over."

Morgan nodded his head in agreement. "You got any more information on Jubal Carver?"

"Our informant still says he's in th' Dog Bark area. That's all he'll say. I do have somethin' else that'll interest you, though. Reynolds shot and killed Karl Woodson two days after you left."

"Is Nolan all right?"

"Not a scratch."

"How'd it happen?"

"I'm not real sure, but, as I hear it, Woodson refused to leave town. When Reynolds pushed the issue, Woodson pulled on him."

"I can't say I'm sorry, but now with him and Farkle both dead…" He stopped as he thought, "now, there's only one who knows…I wonder."

"Any news on Bear Paw?"

McEachern sighed, "Not much. There's been no activity up north that can be tied to him. Latest information has him workin' in this general area. Some of th' army brass think he's been killed."

McEachern handed Morgan a piece of paper, "Here's some information on Piper, Rideout, and Leatherwood. My office is still gatherin' everything they can. I'll get it to you as soon as I can."

Morgan put the paper in his pocket, "Thanks. I've got several more names for you: Burkett, Zachary, Collins, and Treywick." He took out a folded piece of paper with the names on it and gave it to McEachern. "Burkett is a gambler who hangs around Dog Bark and Blackthorn. Zachary punches cows at th' Kiowa Lance. Collins is a deputy here in Griffin. Treywick's a saloon keeper at Blackthorn."

McEachern put the paper in his pocket and asked, "Where does a deputy from Fort Griffin fit into all this?"

"Maybe nowhere. His name just keeps croppin' up."

"I'll get right on it. How can I reach you?"

"I think it's best we don't meet again. It's too dangerous. There's a graveyard at Blackthorn. In th' southwest corner there's a tall headstone. I'll place a rock by th' headstone. We can leave our messages there."

"Sounds like a good idea." He shook Morgan's hand, "You be careful, hear?"

"I aim to."

McEachern was halfway down when Morgan called after him, "Wallace, add one more name to th' list...Joel Crow. Wallace, don't you believe for a second that Bear Paw is dead."

Morgan lay down on the blanket that Asa had spread for him, thinking, "Probably a waste of time. Still, Treywick said he was there." Morgan was tired, but he forced himself to rethink everything that had happened. After he was satisfied he'd covered all angles, he got up and lit the lantern Whitmore had hanging on a nail. Morgan turned down the wick so only a flicker of light was visible; he read the information McEachern had given him and then reread his own notes.

Morgan dowsed the light and thought, "Some of th' picture is clearin' up." He lay down and was asleep in minutes. He dreamed once again of Devlin...Farkle...the Kiowa warrior...and Bear Paw.

Chapter Thirteen

Morgan left Fort Griffin a good hour before the sun came up. He rode slowly south on the eastern side of the main trail until daylight, then pushed Ebon a little faster; he wanted to make the Kiowa Lance by noon. Morgan stopped often, listening for hoof beats, but heard nothing that alarmed him.

He sat with one leg propped across the saddlehorn, pondering, "If Collins is a part of this, he more'n likely found out I was in Griffin. I'm guessin' Piper and Rideout know by now I'm not at Hangin' Tree...maybe I'm readin' too much into this; it might not be like I think at all." He nudged Ebon forward and mused, "And maybe cows fly." He rubbed Ebon's neck and added, "Ebon, always trust your instincts.

Trustin' mine has saved my hide more'n once."

Suddenly Ebon's head came up. Morgan's hand moved instinctively to his six-shooter.

A rider sat his horse not two hundred yards off to Morgan's left. As soon as Morgan saw him, his skin goosebumped, and a cold, sour feeling slid from his heart to his stomach. It was Bear Paw!

"Easy boy, easy," Morgan soothed Ebon, who was dancing nervously. Ebon calmed down immediately at the sound of Morgan's voice. "No sudden moves...he ain't wantin' to fight. If he did, I wouldn't have seen him. He meant for me to see him. I wonder what he wants?" Morgan pressed Ebon with his knees, "Ebon, let's go see what's on his mind."

Bear Paw sat unmoving until Morgan had covered half of the distance between them; then he kneed his paint pony and rode slowly down the hill.

When Morgan reached the top of the knoll, the Kiowa had vanished. Morgan knew he'd seen the last of him for a while. He stepped down, thinking, "I sure ain't goin' after him....I gotta feelin' he wants to talk. He'll get around to it. I'm glad he wants to talk first." Something off to Morgan's left caught his eye, and he walked slowly to toward it. The sour feeling in his stomach returned.

Bear Paw had drawn another crude bear print in the dirt; his signature arrow was stuck in the middle of the print, but this time he had left another arrow stuck in the ground just outside the print. Morgan studied the print and the two arrows and thought, "He's tryin' to tell me somethin'...but what?"

Morgan pulled the arrow from the print and mused, "Just like th' ones at Medicine Lodge...Burl an' Pete...black with three red circles." He pulled the other arrow from the ground, "This one's totally different. What's he tryin' to tell me?" Morgan thought for a moment, and then answered his own questions. "It ain't his doin'. He wants me to know he didn't kill that deputy and those farmers."

Morgan wrapped the arrows in his saddle roll and continued his journey to the Kiowa Lance. His thoughts bounced back and forth from Bear Paw to that day at Medicine Lodge, then to the day he had to kill the Kiowa warrior. They rambled to Jubal Carver, and to Chris Walsh, Piper, Rideout, Leatherwood, Collins…Marshall Reynolds and Farkle…Karl Woodson, and to Jim Bob and Catfish, and, for some reason, to Linda Farquar. He frowned at his last thought and said aloud to himself, "I ain't got th' time."

The sign on a big oak tree read, "Kiowa Lance—Trespassers Will Be Shot—Rustlers, Hung." Morgan read the sign and said, "Ebon, are we trespassers?" The gray gelding nickered quietly. Morgan urged him gently forward, "I don't think so. If we play our cards right, Killpatrick just might provide some of th' answers we want…providin' he'll talk. We'll see. It won't hurt to ask…maybe."

Morgan saw three more no trespassing signs in the next two hours. After another half-hour ride he saw a different sign. It read, "Kiowa Lance," and an arrow pointed southeast. Morgan thought, "Must be for non-trespassers." Ten minutes later, Morgan rode under the tall Kiowa Lance sign that led to the sprawling ranch still barely visible from the entrance. Off to his right he saw three riders coming fast, and mused, "Ebon, we got company." He removed the thong from his Colt and added, "I get th' feelin' they ain't th' welcomin' committee."

The three riders slid their horses to a stop in the middle of the road, then turned to face Morgan. Morgan rode slowly toward them, thinking, "That's Zachary in th' middle. I've never seen the other two." He rode within four feet of them and stopped.

"Can't you read?" said Zachary.

"I'm here to see Killpatrick."

"You ain't seein' nobody," snapped Zachary. "And I asked you a question, Mister."

Morgan moved closer, "Back off while you still can." His eyes were black and hard; his voice was cold.

Zachary smiled weakly, "Not only can't he read, boys; he can't see either. There's three of us."

"There were four of you at th' saloon," Morgan calmly replied.

"That wuz different," sputtered Zachary. "I wuz—"

"A struttin' rooster," interrupted Morgan. "Just like now." The other two cowboys began to nervously move away from Zachary. Morgan continued, "You may have these boys fooled, but I know you for what you are: a lyin', cheatin' coward." Morgan let his challenge sink in.

Zachary cut uneasy eyes right and left, looking for any sign that the cowboys would back him up; he saw only apprehension and fear. He turned back to Morgan, put his shaking hands on his saddle horn and whispered softly, "I didn't see th' badge when you first rode up. If you…" He let his voice fade.

"Uh-huh," Morgan said. The sound of oncoming horses caused Zachary and the two cowboys to swivel in their saddles to see who was approaching. He thought, "This could get sticky."

Zachary turned to Morgan with obvious relief showing on his face. "It's th' ol' man. Your ass is cooked now."

"Is that a fact?"

"Your damn right, it's a fact," sneered Zachary. "You're gonna be talkin' outta th' other side of your face when he gets here."

"Like I said, I came here to talk to Killpatrick."

As the two riders rode up, the older one said, "Carl, what's goin' on here?"

Zachary nodded to Morgan, "Seems we got us a trespasser, Mr. Killpatrick. He's th' one I told you about in th' One-Eyed Jack."

Killpatrick and Morgan's eyes locked. Without looking

away, Killpatrick quietly said, "Ray, Will—y'all get on back to work." Both cowboys turned without a word and rode off. Killpatrick turned his attention to Morgan, "Morgan, what brings you to th' Kiowa Lance?"

Morgan saw a frown creep into Zachary's face and a wry grin appear on the other puncher's lips. "I was hopin' we could have a little talk, Mr. Killpatrick."

Zachary stammered, "I told him—"

Killpatrick held up his hand and cut Zachary off, "That'll be all, Carl." Zachary's face colored.

"But Mr. Kill—"

"I said that'll be all, Carl." Irritation was evident in his voice. Zachary glared at Morgan with pure hatred in his eyes as he dug his spurs into his mount's flanks. The horse squealed, then broke into a dead run away from the group.

Killpatrick shook his head and frowned, then said, "You said you wanted to talk. I'm all ears." Morgan looked at the other cowboy, and Killpatrick added, "This is my foreman, Roy Adcock. Anything you have to say, you can say in front of him."

"All right. Mr. Killpatrick, I'll get right to th' point. I'm lookin' for any information that'll help me get a line on all th' trouble that's sprung up in th' county of late."

"What trouble are you speaking of?" His tone was casual.

"Oh, murder, robbery, bushwhacking, rustling," replied Morgan evenly.

Killpatrick studied Morgan for a moment. "Did Piper send you out here?"

"Nope."

"You're workin' for him, aren't you?"

"Yep."

Killpatrick scratched his chin, "Morgan. I'm just a tad confused. As a matter of fact, there's several things about you that's puzzlin' me."

"Such as?"

"First of all, your reputation precedes you. When Carl told me you were in Dog Bark, I naturally asked myself, 'What's he doin' here?' So I'll ask you. What brings you to Dog Bark?"

Morgan told him of how he was on his way to California and of Reynolds' letter of recommendation. Morgan finished by saying, "and that's th' truth of it."

Killpatrick reflected on Morgan's story for several moments before he said, "Zachary says you stepped in for one of Haggard's wranglers after they had caught him cheatin'. What's your side of it?"

Morgan looked Killpatrick square in the eyes. "He's a liar." Morgan waited for Killpatrick to react to his declaration, but Killpatrick said nothing; he just sat and stared. Morgan then recounted what had happened.

"I see," said Killpatrick. He turned to Adcock, "Roy, that ain't th' way Zachary told it."

"He's tellin' you th' straight of it," answered Adcock. When Killpatrick raised his eyebrows, he added, "Gilkey was there. He told me th' same story Morgan just told."

"Hmmm," said Killpatrick. He turned back to Morgan. "There's this other thing that's queer to my way of thinkin'. Leatherwood and Piper have been thicker'n thieves—"

"Not to mention Rideout," offered Adcock.

Killpatrick shook his head and continued, "Kinda odd, him firin' Leatherwood and givin' you his badge."

"I suppose it does appear that way," replied Morgan. "But he did…for whatever reason."

"Morgan, when I first came out here, there wasn't any law but range law. If you rustled my cattle, stole my horses, I hanged you. You bushwhacked my men, I'd hunt you down. No organized law, mind you. *I* was th' law, and we had justice. Now we got legal law, and my men are bushwhacked, my cattle rustled…" He left his thoughts hanging.

Morgan sensed that Killpatrick wasn't through, so he remained silent.

Killpatrick continued, "I was here when Haggard was just a pup. I was here fightin' Comanche while he was safe back East." He touched his thigh as though it brought him pleasure. "Caught me a Comanche arrow in '68. Still, I let him and those sodbusters come in...never pushed 'em one bit." He pushed his hat back and wiped sweat from his brow with the bandanna he pulled from around his neck, all the while measuring Morgan.

Morgan gave no indication that he was going to interrupt, so Killpatrick went on. "It was me who gave th' name Dog Bark. When I first came, there was an abandoned Comanche camp on th' present site of Dog Bark. They'd left behind an ol' dog. He was barkin' his head off, so I called th' place Dog Bark, and it stuck. And it was me that gave th' name Hangin' Tree...for obvious reasons. There's a big oak tree there. I hung ten, twelve rustlers and four murderin' Comanches from that tree."

Morgan nodded his head in agreement with what Killpatrick had said. "Mr. Killpatrick, what can you tell me about th' two deputies who were killed and th' one that's disappeared?"

Killpatrick's face stiffened and his eyes blazed. "You ain't insinuatin' that I had anything to do with that, are you?"

"No, I ain't."

Killpatrick was mad, and it showed; he stared at Morgan for several moments before saying, "I had no reason to kill those men."

Morgan studied Killpatrick for a moment, nodded his head, and quietly said, "I believe you. Thanks for talkin' with me." He turned to go, but Killpatrick stopped him.

"Morgan, tell Piper I'm not waitin' on him th' next time my men are shot at, or my cattle stolen. I'm gonna take care of it myself."

Morgan turned back and faced Killpatrick. "Mr. Killpatrick, I wish you wouldn't do that. It's my job." He paused and added in a calm voice, "And I aim to do it." Morgan turned and rode slowly away.

The two men sat quietly and watched Morgan go. Killpatrick spoke first. "Roy, what do you make of him?"

Adcock pondered the question, then replied, "He's got a lot of bark on him; that's for sure."

"Yeah, but there's somethin' else, too."

"That Colt looks right at home on his hip. Did you notice he was packin' a Winchester and a Sharps?"

"I saw," answered Killpatrick. "But there's something else. It's a feelin' I got."

"Maybe it's those eyes...black as midnight. Looks like he's seein' plumb through you."

Killpatrick slapped the reins nervously against his leg, "It was th' way he was talkin'—not like an ordinary deputy...like he was talkin' for himself, and not for Piper. Yet, he's Piper's deputy—"

"I know one thing," Adcock said. "He's got some Injun in him from somewhere down th' line."

"Comanche," replied Killpatrick. He flicked the reins nervously several more times and asked, "Mr. Morgan, who are you?" He turned to Adcock. "Texas Ranger? Maybe—I got a feelin' we'll know pretty soon."

Chapter Fourteen

Morgan left Killpatrick and Adcock, thinking, "That ol' man's about half rank...be a good man to have on your side when push comes to shove. I've got a gut feelin' he's tellin' th' truth. If that's th' case, only two things come to mind. Either Haggard's tryin' to be number one, or someone's in th' middle, playin' both sides. If that's so, everything points to Piper and Rideout...Leatherwood? Where's Jubal Carver fit into this puzzle? Maybe he don't. He ain't even here...and who's leanin' on th' farmers? Only thing I'm reasonably sure of is Bear Paw ain't a part of this...yet."

Morgan urged Ebon faster and mused, "Ebon, just listen to me, jumpin' to conclusions I can't prove. Even if it is them…why? Killin' Walsh and those deputies…stakes must be mighty high, and that's a fact."

Morgan headed for Dog Bark to play a hunch. He stopped at his hiding place and placed his and McEachern's notes along with his U.S. Marshall badge and letter of appointment. "Ain't no sense in takin' a chance. I've been lucky so far. Sooner or later someone's gonna put two and two together; I've gotta be ready when they do."

Morgan found a secluded spot about a quarter of a mile from Dog Bark and waited for darkness. When it was fully dark, he walked slowly to town. "No moon tonight. I might just get lucky and hear, or see, somethin'."

Morgan circled Dog Bark so he could approach from the west, coming up behind the hotel. He climbed quickly to the roof and crept quietly to the front balcony. He thought through the town's layout. "Th' One-Eyed Jack is just across th' street…sheriff's office is not far. If I'm to find out anything, this is th' best vantage point." He settled in, determined to stay all night, if necessary.

After over an hour of futile watching and listening, Morgan was beginning to think he'd played a bad hunch; he neither saw nor heard anything of interest—only a few cowboys entering and leaving the saloon and diners leaving the hotel. Suddenly he heard a familiar voice.

"Crow, how many times do I haf'ta tell ya?" The bat-wings flew open as Rideout shoved Joel Crow out into the street. "Go sleep it off…" Rideout's voice faded, then came back. "Goddamned drunk." Laughter floated out of the saloon and into the night air.

Morgan watched Crow stagger to his feet and thought, "Every time I see him, he's drunker'n Cooter Brown." Morgan watched Crow weave to the alley. The next sound he heard caused him to say, "What th'…?"

He cut his words short as he thought, "A drunk pourin' out

whiskey? That's strange…real strange." He watched Crow until the shadows of the alley engulfed him.

Morgan's thoughts concerning Crow were replaced by those of Rideout and Leatherwood as they came out of the saloon and headed toward him. Morgan couldn't make out what they were saying at first, but when the two reached the middle of the street, he heard Rideout say, "I told you if you played your cards right, you'd get your badge back, didn't I?"

"Yeah, you told me," growled Leatherwood. "Now I'm tellin' you…I ain't gonna sit around on my hands any longer. I'm gonna go get that son of a bitch." They had reached the boardwalk and were directly below Morgan.

Rideout sighed, "You're hell bent on gettin' yourself killed. I told—"

"Ain't gonna be no gun play," interrupted Tiny. "I'm gonna break every bone in that breed's body."

"Morgan ain't no fool. He ain't gonna stand there and let you beat on him. He's gonna blow your brains out."

"No way. I know his kind; he's got pride. He'll fight." As they walked toward the sheriff's office, Morgan could only hear snatches of their conversation. "Does Piper know where…Morgan?"

Then from Rideout, "In Blackthorn…Collins…Griffin… out at th' Kiowa Lance—"

Morgan watched them enter the sheriff's office, thinking, "At least I know where Collins stands, but how'd they know I was at th' Kiowa Lance?" He thought for a moment and then answered his own question, "Zachary! Th' players are beginnin' to fall into place. But th' whys…wherefors…"

Morgan watched Doc O'Banion leave the One-Eyed Jack and climb the stairs to his office over the *Dog Bark Clarion*, and thought, "Now's a good time to ask him some questions." He dropped quietly to the ground behind the hotel and made his way to O'Banion's office; Morgan waited several minutes beneath the stairs, making sure that no one had followed or seen him. He slipped quickly up the stairs and knocked softly on the door.

"Who's there?" called O'Banion.

"Stuart Morgan," whispered Morgan.

O'Banion opened the door. "Are you hurt?"

Morgan stepped quickly in, shut the door, and pulled down the shade. "No. I just wanna talk."

"Are you running from someone?"

"Nothin' like that, Doc. I just think it best we talk in private."

O'Banion studied Morgan for a brief moment. "All right. What about?"

"I was wonderin' if you examined th' bodies of th' two deputies who were killed."

"Yes, I did."

"Did you find anything unusual?"

O'Banion scratched his head and thought back. "That depends on what you consider unusual. Harvey Pickett was shot in the back with an arrow."

"Was he scalped?"

"No, he wasn't. The only wound I found on him was the one made by the arrow; it punctured his heart. That Indian is good with that bow."

A frown creased Morgan's face. "Doc, you wouldn't by chance remember what that arrow looked like, would you?"

O'Banion walked over to his desk. "See for yourself." He rummaged through the desk drawer, found the arrow, and handed it to Morgan.

Morgan took the arrow and thought, "It's not him. This one is a dead ringer for th' other one Bear Paw left outside his bear track...so that's what he's tryin' to tell me."

"Mind if I keep this?"

"No, not at all."

Morgan studied the arrow for a moment longer, then asked, "What about th' other deputy?"

"Gill Warner was shot in the back." O'Banion lowered his voice and added, "Probably by someone he knew."

Morgan frowned, "Someone he knew?"

"Well, that's my way of thinking. There were powder burns on his shirt, and his gun was still in his holster."

"Any ideas on th' gun used to kill him?"

"Forty-five. I've got the slug here somewhere. If you—"

Morgan waved his hand, "That ain't necessary, Doc. Thanks for th' information." Morgan stepped to the door, peeked under the drawn shade, and said, "Doc, I'd appreciate it if we kept our little talk between th' two of us."

O'Banion was caught up in thoughts of the way Morgan's eyes seemed to go from dark to pitch black. He didn't answer right away; he finally said, "If that's the way you want it."

Morgan nodded his head. "Be seein' ya, Doc."

O'Banion locked the door behind Morgan and mused, "That fuse is getting shorter."

Morgan stayed the night where he had left Ebon; he spent much of the remaining night thinking and rethinking all of the information that he had compiled. He finally dozed, thinking, "I'm way ahead of where I was a week ago. Things are startin' to fall into place and make sense, I think."

At daybreak, Morgan started for the Circle H. "Ebon, what's th' best way to bring down two big grizzlies? Only a fool would try to whip both of 'em at once. One way is to figure out how to get 'em goin' at each other, then set back and let 'em wear on each other...then, when there's only one left, or when both are wore down...step in and take 'em." Morgan patted Ebon's neck, "I think that's what someone is tryin' to do to Killpatrick and Haggard."

Morgan had been on the Circle H range for more than an

hour when he heard sounds of cattle coming out of a draw to his right. "Sounds like a calf that's strayed from his mother…or hurt." He turned Ebon toward the sounds. "Ebon, let's check it out."

Morgan rode into a clearing and thought, "I was right. It is a calf, but it ain't strayed. Someone's brandin'." He studied the tied calf, the nearby fire, and the branding iron, thinking, "Looks like I interrupted—" The sounds of horses coming on fast caused Morgan to break his train of thought. He released the thong from the hammer of his Colt, thinking, "I've got a feelin' I've been set up."

Three cowboys rode into the clearing with pistols drawn. Morgan recognized Rafael Chacon; the other two he didn't know.

"I told you I heard somethin'," growled one cowboy. "Looks like we finally caught one of Killpatrick's rustlers."

The other cowboy said, "Chacon, check that brandin' iron." He cocked his six-shooter and said to Morgan, "Get them hands up."

Morgan raised his hands. "Boys, I'm Deputy Sheriff Stuart Morgan from Dog Bark."

"I don't giv'a shit if you're Wyatt Earp," sneered the first cowboy. "We caught you red-handed." He cocked his pistol and added, "And that means a hangin' is in order."

Chacon put the branding iron he was holding back in the fire and quietly said in broken English, "There will be no hanging. This hombre is no rustler; he saved my life."

The Mexican climbed back on his horse and rode slowly over to Morgan's side. He still held his pistol in his hand.

"What th' hell are you doin', Chacon?" fumed the first cowboy. "You must have shit in your eyes. A blind man could—"

Morgan slowly lowered his arms and hands. "He's tellin' th' truth," interrupted Morgan in a calm voice. "I ain't a rustler. I'm th' law, and I'm gonna say this one time: holster those six-guns."

The second cowboy showed signs of indecision and started to holster his gun which caused the first cowboy to snarl, "Keep it out, Stick. It's still two against one .."

"Two against two," said Chacon. "I tol' you he no rustler."

A heavy silence followed Chacon's declaration. Stick finally said, "Hell, Wesley, he is wearin' a badge." He put his gun away and added, "I ain't goin' against th' law."

Wesley slowly holstered his pistol. "He may be th' law, but it don't mean he ain't workin' a hot iron."

"Easy enough to prove," Morgan said. "I just rode up before y'all got here...ain't even stepped down."

"What th' hell does that prove?" snapped Wesley.

"It proves I'm not th' one who tied that calf." He pointed to the calf and continued, "Check th' tracks around th' calf and th' fire. Your rustler was wearin' high heel boots. Mine are flat."

Stick dismounted and walked to the calf. "He's right, Jones; nothin' but high heels."

"All right. All right," growled Jones. "Untie that damned calf and bring along that Kiowa Lance brandin' iron. Haggard'll want to see it." He jerked his horse around and rode away.

Morgan turned to Chacon, "Thanks, amigo."

Chacon nodded his head, "You come to see Señor Haggard, no?"

"Yes. Will you take me to him?"

"Sí, señor. Señor Haggard, he is but a mile from here. It will be a pleasure to take you to him."

Stick rode over to Morgan and stuck out his hand, "Stick Mason, Morgan. I'm sorry 'bout jumpin' to conclusions." He nodded his head in the direction that Jones had gone and added, "Pay no never mind to Wesley. He don't mean no harm. He's just always hot under th' collar...sees a rustler under ever' rock and an Indian behind ever' tree."

Morgan shook his hand and casually said, "Mind if I see

th' brandin' iron?"

"No, not at all." Mason handed Morgan the iron. "Looks like one of Killpatrick's."

Morgan nodded his head, "Maybe, maybe not." He thought, "Jones said Kiowa Lance brandin' iron. How'd he know it was a Kiowa Lance iron without gettin' down to see?" Morgan dismounted and studied the area as Chacon and Mason watched.

When Morgan was through with his search, Chacon asked, "You find something, no?"

"Maybe, maybe not." Morgan climbed on Ebon and added, "Let's go see Haggard."

"This might be th' last straw," said Mason. "Haggard's about had his fill of Killpatrick."

"Does he have any proof Killpatrick's causin' th' trouble?" Morgan casually asked.

Mason pulled up his horse, "Proof! Who else could it be?"

"They're sayin' th' same thing over at th' Kiowa Lance," Morgan replied. He turned to Mason. "Who are we to believe with both spreads pointin' fingers at one another?"

Mason sputtered, "It sure as hell ain't us. I know Haggard. I've been with him from th' get-go."

"Could be it ain't either one of you," Morgan quietly said.

"Naw, I don't buy that. Hell, ain't nobody else stands to gain anything." Mason then looked at Morgan, "You know somethin' we don't?"

"Nope, not yet. I know from experience though, things are seldom as they appear."

The three rode the rest of the way with Mason doing most of the talking; he informed Morgan of all the things he already knew plus a few he didn't. The more Mason talked about the troubles that had befallen the Circle H; the more Morgan was convinced that his theory was correct.

Mason was saying, "Rustlin', and burnin' line shacks is one thing, but this bushwhackin' is pure bull-shit."

"How many Circle H punchers have been shot at?" asked Morgan.

"Oh, hell, all of us at one time or t'other." Mason then said to Chacon, "Ain't that right, Rafael?"

Chacon shrugged his shoulders as though he didn't understand. Morgan asked Chacon the same question in Spanish; Chacon frowned and answered in Spanish, "I dunno… two…maybe."

"What did he say?" asked Mason.

"He said you were right." Morgan casually asked, "Have you been shot at?"

"Well, no, I've been lucky, but nearly all th' rest have. Why, just last week Wesley came in with a hole in his hat. Ain't that right, Chacon?"

Chacon smiled, "Sí, señor." Then he said in Spanish, "Sometimes he tells tales."

"What did he say?" asked Mason.

"He was tellin' me about Jones," answered Morgan. "Speakin' of Jones, he's a dead ringer for a cowboy I once knew. Where's Jones from, Arkansas?"

"Naw. Wesley's from Sedalia, Missouri; that's all he talks about. He says th' next time Haggard moves a herd to Sedalia, he's gonna stay there."

"How long has Jones been with Haggard?"

"Hell, let me think." Mason thought for a moment, then said, "A year this past March. Yep. It was March."

Before Morgan could reply, Chacon said, "We're here, señor."

As they rode up, Jones said, "That's him, Mr. Haggard." They walked over and Haggard said, "Let me see that brandin' iron."

Mason handed it to him. "It's a Kiowa Lance iron."

"I got eyes," snapped Haggard as another cowboy came up. He tossed the branding iron to the newcomer, "What'd I tell ya, Dub. By god, that tears it."

"It'd be easy enough for someone to steal and plant that iron," Morgan quietly said.

"So you're Morgan," Haggard said. "I hear you've been spendin' a lot of time at th' Kiowa Lance." The tone of his voice made his statement sound like a challenge.

Morgan replied calmly, "Well, you heard wrong, Mr. Haggard."

"You're denying you were there?"

"I didn't say I hadn't been there. I'm sayin' I haven't spent a lot of time there."

Morgan's calm demeanor and voice took some of the fire from Haggard's eyes. He glared at Morgan for a moment and said, "What kind of lies did Killpatrick tell you 'bout me?"

"Nary a one. He's as concerned as you are. Says his cattle are bein' stolen…hands are bein' bushwhacked…mysterious fires and th' like."

Haggard scoffed, "He's blowin' smoke. He ain't foolin' me. He's after my spread, and I'll believe that all th' way to my grave." He paused for a moment and continued. "You didn't ride out here for your health. What do you want?"

"Same as I wanted from Killpatrick—information."

Haggard laughed, "Information! Hell, son, I told Luther months ago what was goin' on. It's past th' information point. From now on I'm gonna protect my property and my men with lead."

Morgan's eyes turned pitch black, and his voice was somber. "Mr. Haggard, it's never too late to try to head off needless killin's. I'll tell you like I told Killpatrick; I'm gonna get to th' bottom of all this. I'm askin' for you not to take th' law into your own hands…I need a little time."

Haggard cocked his head to one side and whispered, "Time. I'm plumb outta time, Morgan. You can tell Piper he had his chance. From now on…" His voice trailed off.

"I'm sorry you feel that way, Mr. Haggard. If you go

outside of th' law, then I'll be comin' for you."

"Is that a threat?"

"No. It's a fact." Morgan turned to leave, but turned again and asked, "What can you tell me about th' three deputies who—"

"Not a damn thing," interrupted Haggard. "Why don't you ask Killpatrick?"

"I did," said Morgan. He rode slowly away.

Haggard watched Morgan ride away, thinking, "Where in th' hell does he fit in? First, he steps in for Chacon, then spends time with Killpatrick. Jones finds him with my calf..." He turned to Jones, "I thought you said he spent th' day at Killpatrick's."

"That's what I heard," stammered Jones.

"You heard? From who?"

"Rideout was talkin' to Tiny at th' cantina in Hangin' Tree. I heard 'em."

Haggard thought for a moment and turned to his foreman, "Dub, Morgan changes th' complexion. Think he means what he said?"

Dub Little moved to Haggard's side. "Uh-huh. Ever' word of it."

Chapter Fifteen

Morgan was halfway to Hanging Tree before it came to him. "It was there all th' time; I just couldn't see it. They've got a man at each spread. Zachary at th' Kiowa Lance and Jones at th' Circle H. They're feedin' 'em information...keepin' th' pot boilin'. Mason said Jones hired on a little over a year ago. That's about th' time all of th' trouble started. I'm bettin' Zachary joined Killpatrick about th' same time. It'd be interestin' to know where Jones and Zachary were when th' bushwhackin' and rustlin' took place, and th' fires were set."

Morgan stopped under an oak tree and took a long drink from his canteen; as he screwed on the cap, he thought, "Knowin' it is one thing, but provin' it is another. Mason said

Jones was from Sedalia, Missouri...that's twice recently...
where else?" Then he remembered. "McEachern's notes!
Rideout or Leatherwood or both are from Sedalia...now we're
gettin' somewhere; it's startin' to make sense."

Morgan's mind was racing. There was something else;
something he'd heard or read. He remounted, thinking, "It'll
come to me...damn! It's irritatin'. What was it? Maybe..."
Then he remembered. "The *Clarion*! Witherspoon's 'Dog
Bark's Newest Barks.' Someone else said he was from
Missouri...who was it? Piper! But it wasn't Sedalia; it was...it
was Kansas City...Kansas City, Missouri."

He urged Ebon forward. "Ebon, what are th' odds of it
bein' just a coincidence? All those fellas showin' up in Texas,
and all of 'em from Missouri." He patted Ebon and continued,
"I wonder what th' odds are on Collins and Burkett bein' from
Missouri...or say, Kansas? Ebon, I'll bet you a double ration
of oats they're from Missouri or Kansas."

Morgan doubled back on his trail and thought, "It ain't gonna
matter what I know if I get careless. Whoever killed those three
deputies ain't gonna hesitate to add me to th' list." He found
a hidden spot and waited. While he was watching and listening, Morgan's mind raced, "I think I know who, but I don't
know why. I gotta figure out a plan to get 'em to tip their hand.
I wonder..." A plan began to formulate in Morgan's mind.

It was dark when Morgan reached Hanging Tree, but even
in the dark he could see that it wasn't much of a town. "Only
see three lights...five or six buildings." He rode slowly in,
thinking, "Treywick was right. Blackthorn is Kansas City
compared to Hangin' Tree. Ain't a soul in sight. I only see
three horses. That must be th' cantina and whorehouse Piper
spoke of."

Morgan slid off Ebon in front of the cantina and tied him
to the hitching post while scrutinizing the three horses. "I've
never seen 'em before. Two of 'em are U.S. Army." He took

the thong from the hammer of his Colt. "I've got that feelin' again, and I ain't usually wrong."

The only people Morgan saw were all sitting at one table far in the back. As Morgan walked to the bar, a tall, thin, swarthy man left the two women and went behind the bar. "I'm Mendoza. Morgan, ain't it? I been wonderin' when you'd get around to visitin' us."

Morgan was looking at the two women as he asked, "Do you know me?"

"Nope, but you are Morgan ain't you?"

"I'm Morgan." He was thinking, "They must be upstairs." He turned to Mendoza, "Where're your three customers?"

Mendoza grinned and nodded his head toward the stairs, "Upstairs. They're being entertained. I've got two left. You can take your pick."

"What are their names?"

"Rosa and Maria." He leaned toward Morgan, lowered his voice, and added, "If I wuz you, I'd take Rosa. She—"

Morgan cut him off, "I was referrin' to th' men."

Mendoza frowned, "Oh, them."

"Yeah, them."

"One of 'em is Louis Garza from th' Circle H. Th' other two are troopers from Fort Griffin…didn't catch their names." He took a bottle of whiskey from under the bar, "Th' first drink is on th' house. Th' law—"

"This ain't no social call," interrupted Morgan. "I'm investigatin' th' murder of Gill Warner."

Mendoza's face stiffened. "Warner…oh, yeah, th' deputy."

"Was he in here th' night he was killed?"

Mendoza nervously picked up a towel and began rubbing the bar, "Damn, that was over a year ago. Maybe he wuz; maybe he wasn't. I don't remember."

Morgan's eyes turned black and hard. "Were you workin' that night?"

"Yeah. I wuz…" He realized Morgan had trapped him and covered, "Now I remember. He was here."

"Now that your memory is back, who else was here?"

Mendoza's hands were shaking, and his eyes were wide. His mind was racing trying to think of what to say. All the while Morgan's eyes kept boring holes into him. He finally stammered, "Geez…been so long. I dunno—"

Morgan reached over and pulled Mendoza hard into the bar. "Mendoza, my patience is wearin' mighty thin. You're right on th' edge. Now, I asked you a question."

"Now I remember," sputtered Mendoza. Morgan shoved him back from the bar. Mendoza continued in a voice that sounded unused and hollow. "I think some of th' Circle H hands were here, and maybe one or two from th' Kiowa Lance."

Morgan stared at Mendoza for several seconds. Mendoza looked away. "Look at me when I'm talkin' to you." Mendoza looked timidly at Morgan, and Morgan continued, "Name names."

Mendoza was visibly shaken as he whispered, "Mason… Jones…maybe Chacon, I think."

"Who else?" asked Morgan. "You said th' Kiowa Lance."

Mendoza rolled his eyes. "Yeah, I did. I'm tryin' to remember…it wuz—"

"Carl Zachary," said Morgan.

Morgan's revelation caused Mendoza to shake harder, and he stammered weakly, "Come to think of it, he wuz here."

Morgan decided to play a hunch. "And th' deputies from Dog Bark were here, too, weren't they?"

Sweat was now pouring down Mendoza's face as he struggled to formulate an answer to Morgan's statement and question. He wiped at the sweat and stuttered, "I-I-I'm not sure. I couldn't swear to it."

"They were here," said one of the whores. "Tiny still owes me two dollars from that night."

The other whore giggled, "Rosa, you ain't ever gonna get that two dollars. He owes every workin' girl here money."

Morgan turned back to Mendoza, "Is it comin' back to you?"

Mendoza stared hard at Rosa and Maria, then smiled faintly at Morgan, "Yeah, now I remember. I believe they were here. But, like I say, I can't swear to it."

Morgan glowered at Mendoza, "Uh-huh. You can't swear to it." He moved to Rosa and Maria, "Ladies, I'm Stuart Morgan, deputy from Dog Bark."

"I do declare," replied Rosa. "Maria, are you as surprised as I am?"

"About what?" asked Maria.

"I thought he'd be at least ten feet tall." She smiled at Morgan and raised her eyebrows. "All I've heard these last two or three days is 'Morgan, Morgan.'" She cocked her head to one side and asked, "Did you really whip Tiny?"

Morgan grinned, "Let's just say he was sleepin' when I left th' One-Eyed Jack."

Rosa cackled, "I'd give ten dollars to see that slob layin' on th' floor."

Maria nodded her head toward Mendoza, "Shhhh…if Tiny finds out what you're sayin', he'll—"

Rosa waved her off, "Who cares? Th' hell with Tiny…th' hell with all of 'em."

Morgan nodded to one of the empty chairs, "May I?"

"Sure. Why not?" replied Rosa.

Morgan chose the chair that would allow him to sit with his back to the wall and see the entire cantina. He placed his hat on the table and said casually to Rosa, "You said th' deputies from Dog Bark were here th' night Warner was killed?"

"Are you gonna buy us a drink?" Rosa smiled. "House rules."

Morgan held up two fingers to Mendoza. "Two drinks for th' ladies."

"Well looka here!" exclaimed Rosa. "Th' law buyin' us a drink."

"Did Leatherwood and Rideout buy you a drink th' night Warner was killed?"

The two women burst out laughing. "Now that's funny," Rosa said. Her face stiffened, and her eyes glittered hotly as she added, "Buy us a drink? Those bastards? They think cause they're th' law they can lay with us for free. Does that sound like they'd buy us drinks?"

"No, I guess not," replied Morgan as Mendoza brought the drinks. Morgan waited until he'd gone back to the bar, then continued, "What do you remember about that night?"

Rosa tossed her drink down in one quick swallow and wiped her mouth with the back of her hand, "They were here before Warner showed up…went out th' back door just before he came in."

"Rideout and Leatherwood?"

Rosa shook her head, "Uh-huh."

Maria added, "They left right after Carl came in and told them somethin'."

"Carl Zachary?"

Maria nodded her head, and Rosa said, "It was him…he's always with 'em. If you want my opinion, he's as big of an ass as them two."

"Bigger," spat Maria. She touched her nose, "He hit me, broke my nose, just cause I told him I was sick and couldn't do it with him. Called me a fuckin' whore."

Morgan changed the subject. "I'm a little confused, ladies. I'm a Dog Bark deputy…just like Rideout and Leatherwood—"

Before Morgan could finish, Rosa interrupted. "But you ain't one of 'em."

"How's that?"

"Cause we heard 'em say you weren't," answered Maria.

Morgan's heart jumped. "You heard 'em talkin' 'bout me?"

"Uh-huh. Day before yesterday…when they were here," said Rosa.

"They were here and waitin' on me. I'm glad I went to Blackthorn…this removes all doubt," he thought. "Did they know you were listenin'?"

Maria shook her head, "No."

"They were in Polly's room. We were next door, in my room. Th' walls are paper thin," said Rosa.

"What'd you hear?"

"Just pieces. We couldn't hear everything they said, but I heard them say your name. Tiny said, 'Jack, he ain't on th' level,' whatever that means," commented Rosa.

Maria said, "One of 'em said he was gonna kill you. I think it was Tiny…Jack said somethin' about a Texas Ranger, and somethin' about Sheriff Piper. I couldn't make it out. We didn't know who they were talkin' about 'til Stick and Rafael told us what you did to Tiny."

"And about you shamin' Wesley," grinned Rosa.

Morgan heard voices at the top of the stairs. "Maybe I can get a message to Coldiron by th' soldiers." He put on his hat and said, "I'm obliged for th' information…I'd appreciate it if you'd keep our conversation between th' three of us."

"Don't worry," replied Rosa. "We ain't gonna tell 'em th' time of day." Maria nodded her head in agreement.

Morgan touched the brim of his hat. "Thanks. Be seein' ya."

Morgan placed a dollar in front of Mendoza and softly said, "Mendoza, if I hear later that your memory 'bout me bein' here is better than it was th' night Warner was killed…or you develop a case of th' slack jaw—"

"I ain't never laid eyes on you," sputtered Mendoza.

Morgan glowered at Mendoza for several moments, and calmly said, "I thought you'd see it my way."

"I don't want no trouble," he whined.

Morgan nodded his head, went to the end of the bar, and hurriedly wrote a note to Coldiron. He then went outside to wait for the two soldiers; while he was waiting, he thought "Maybe he can find out for me…" His thoughts were interrupted by the soldiers, who came noisily out the door. Morgan folded his note and said, "Evenin'. I'd like a word with you."

The tall soldier wearing sergeant's stripes eyed Morgan's badge and asked, "What about?"

"I'm Stuart Morgan. I was wonderin' if you'd take a message to Captain Coldiron for me?"

The sergeant studied Morgan for a moment in the dim light of the cantina, then asked, "Are you th' Morgan th' Captain's always talkin' about?"

A smile creased Morgan's face, "I reckon I am."

The sergeant stuck out his hand, "Sergeant Crosby, Morgan." He nodded to the other soldier, "This here's Private Willcox." Morgan shook Willcox's hand as Crosby continued, "Th' captain speaks highly of you. Any friend of his is a friend of ours. You said you had a message for Captain Coldiron."

Morgan handed the note to Crosby, "If it's no trouble?"

Crosby put the note in his pocket, "No trouble at all. Anything else I can do for you?"

"Naw, that's it."

Crosby grinned, "I wuz wonderin' if you'd do us a favor."

"All right."

Crosby's grin widened, "Don't tell th' Captain where you saw us." He nodded to the cantina and added, "We're on duty…returnin' from Fort Concho."

"Coldiron's still goin' by th' book," chuckled Morgan.

"You know it," said Willcox. "If he finds out, our ass'll be in a sling."

"And that's th' straight of it," added Crosby.

"It's between th' three of us," Morgan smiled.

As the soldiers rode off, Rosa came out on the boardwalk. "Thanks for th' drink." She smiled, raised her eyebrows, and asked, "Is there anything I can do for you?"

Morgan knew what she meant; he climbed on Ebon and smiled as he said, "Maybe next time."

Rosa stepped out to the hitching rail and patted Ebon, all the while staring into Morgan's eyes. She finally said quietly, "You ain't th' kind. There ain't gonna be no next time, is there?"

Morgan was thinking, "She's probably no more than thirty...looks forty. Her eyes are old, washed out, faded, like th' dress. What makes 'em do this?"

"Rosa, you've got me figured. I ain't th' kind...no offense intended."

She smiled weakly, "I didn't think so." She turned and walked slowly to the cantina. When she reached the door, she turned to Morgan and added, "Too bad. It would've been th' best you ever had."

Morgan had a wry smile upon his face as he rode out of Hanging Tree; then the smile thinned and finally faded entirely as his thoughts returned to the matters at hand.

As was his practice, Morgan avoided the traveled trail. He was going to Dog Bark, and he was in no hurry; he had decided to spend two days in the brush before going on to Dog Bark. Morgan wanted to give Coldiron and McEachern some time to gather the information he needed; besides, he had some thinking to do.

He rode for an hour or so, found a suitable spot, and camped for the night. Just before he dozed off, he thought, "I'm probably safer in Dog Bark than anywhere else...they ain't gonna risk killin' me there. Dry-gulching on th' trail is more'n likely their plan, but I can't be cat-hair sure 'bout nothin' with those pole cats."

Chapter Sixteen

Three days later, before daylight, a light shown in the window of Dog Bark's county sheriff's office. Luther Piper refilled his coffee cup and said, "Tiny, you ain't gonna do nothin' 'less I tell you to."

"Hell, Luther. He's just a man," said Tiny. "If y'all had listened to me—"

"We wouldn't be listenin' to you now," smirked Rideout.

"What th' hell does that mean?" asked Tiny.

Rideout sighed, "Luther, you explain it to him."

Tiny turned to Piper, "Explain what?"

Piper frowned, "Damn it, Tiny…Jack's tryin' to tell ya. I'm tryin' to tell ya. Morgan ain't just a man. You go off half-cocked with him, and he's gonna kill ya. Besides, we don't know who he's workin' for."

"We shoulda killed him that first day," grumbled Tiny.

"Yeah, boy," replied Rideout. "That would've been real smart."

"Jack, I'm gettin' pretty damn tired of you always sayin' I'm dumb," said Tiny. "One of these days I'm gonna—"

"Cut that shit out," snapped Piper. "Damnit t' hell. We got enough problems…" He let his voice trail off, took a sip of his coffee, and continued, "Until I can find out more about Morgan, let's play it quiet for a while. Jack, get word to Zachary and Jones. Tell 'em everything's off, 'til I tell 'em otherwise." He turned to Leatherwood, "Tiny, ride over to Fort Griffin, tell Collins I wanna see him." He drained his cup and added, "I'll tell Burkett."

Leatherwood got up, jammed his hat on his head, and moved to the door, grumbling, "I had my mind set on goin' to Hangin' Tree…gettin' me some."

Piper called after him, "Remember what I said. If you run into Morgan, stay th' hell away from him. You hear?"

"Yeah, I—well looka here." Tiny stepped back to Piper and Rideout. "Speakin' of th' devil, Morgan's on his way over."

"Morgan!" exclaimed Rideout. "He's here?"

"Bigger'n damnit," grinned Tiny.

"Y'all keep your yaps shut," ordered Piper. "I'll handle this."

Morgan stepped in and quietly said, "Mornin'."

"Mornin'," replied Piper. "How's things at Blackthorn and Hangin' Tree?"

"Pretty quiet. Not much happenin'." Morgan stared at Leatherwood and added, "I see there's been some changes here."

Piper acted as though he didn't know what Morgan was talking about. "Naw, things are quiet, real quiet."

Rideout chuckled, "It's so quiet, you can hear a mouse pissin' on cotton way over at th' general store."

Morgan smiled faintly, "Well, to be honest, it ain't been that quiet." He told them of his run-in with Jim Bob and Catfish, knowing all the time they already knew of it. Morgan finished by saying, "I ran 'em outta Blackthorn, told 'em not to come back to th' county."

"You did right. Why'd they jump you?" asked Piper.

"Can't rightly say," Morgan deadpanned. "Said they mistook me for someone else."

"You sure musta stepped on a lotta toes up in Fort Worth," said Rideout. "I can kinda understand though. You ain't th' friendliest fella I ever met."

"It's been said of me," replied Morgan. He said to Piper, "Just wanted to check in with ya. I'm gonna pick up some supplies…goin' to Blackthorn this afternoon. You got anything you want me to do?"

Piper waved his hand, "Naw. You're doin' fine. Just keep th' lid on those two festerin' hellholes."

Morgan nodded his head, "Be seein' ya." He passed Tiny and said, "You're lookin' a little bit better'n th' last time I saw you." Morgan smiled to himself as he saw the anger and hatred jump into Leatherwood's eyes.

He closed the door, thinking, "That oughta get it goin'. If I was a bettin' man…they'll try somethin' in th' next day or two. I gotta be ready. I'll be real surprised if one of 'em don't leave town today."

"That's one cool bastard," announced Rideout. "I wonder where he's been these past two days?"

"That he is; that he is," replied Piper. "I get th' feelin' he knows a lot more'n he's lettin' on. I still can't put it together…him showin' up here with th' letter from Reynolds."

"You fucked up in hirin' him," said Tiny. "Hell, I coulda killed him, or—"

Piper interrupted, "No, hirin' him was th' smart thing to do. At least this way we can sorta keep an eye on him."

"You got a plan?" asked Rideout.

"Maybe. I'm gonna do a little more checkin'. I've sent wires to some friends of mine. Should know somethin' in a couple of days. Meanwhile we're gonna lay low; let him make th' first move."

"A coupl'a days," whined Tiny. "Luther, let me—"

"Go to Fort Griffin like I told you," interrupted Piper.

Leatherwood stomped to the door and slammed it so hard the entire building rattled. "Th' boy ain't never gonna learn," Rideout said.

"No, I reckon he ain't. But it don't matter 'cause he's just about used up his usefulness."

"I was thinkin' th' same thing." Rideout grinned. "Maybe Morgan'll do us a favor."

Piper shook his head, "Th' problem with that is th' fool'd probably end up tellin' Morgan everything he knows." Piper drummed his fingers on the desk top and stared off in space for several moments before saying, "When he gets back from Griffin…" Piper raised his eyebrows, cocked his head to one side and whispered, "I think it's time Tiny had a little accident."

Rideout smiled wickedly, "I'll take care of it."

Morgan took Ebon to the livery, then went to the hotel for breakfast. Afterwards he had a bath and shave at Seth's Barber Shop. He left the barber shop, thinking, "Maybe I'll get lucky. It's a long shot, but…" He went into the telegraph office and said to the telegrapher, "Mornin'. I need some information."

The telegrapher was a small, balding man with spectacles. He smiled nervously, "Mornin', Mr. Morgan. You wanna send a wire?"

"Nope, just some information. Do you keep records on incomin' and outgoin' messages?"

The little man beamed, "Company policy. I log ever' one of 'em. Whatcha wanna know?"

"What came in and out on...let's see...twelve and thirteen May?"

The telegrapher reached under the counter and retrieved his log book. He turned the pages and said, "Here we are... twelve May...three incoming...two outgoin'. The first one was for Bob McCowan." He looked up and added, "Bob's th' mayor, owns McCowan's Dry Goods. Th' second one was for Luther, and, let's see...th' last one was for Crow."

Morgan frowned, "The drunk?"

"Only Crow in Dog Bark."

"Where'd th' wires come from?"

The telegrapher looked again at his log, "Luther, Austin. McCowan...Kansas City. Crow...that's strange...I didn't write it down...that's odd."

Morgan scratched his chin and asked, "How 'bout th' outgoin'?"

"Piper...to Austin. McCowan to Kansas City."

Morgan pondered on the information for a moment, then asked, "What've you got for the thirteenth?"

He ran his finger down the log and replied, "Four and four. Let's see...Doc O'Banion, McCowan, Miz Farquar, and Seth. Outgoin...O'Banion, Witherspoon, Farquar, and Burkett."

"Where'd you send Burkett's wire?"

The telegrapher squinted his eyes as he read the log, "Damn! Can't read my own writin'. I think...yes, now I remember...Washington D.C."

Morgan took out his notepad and wrote hurriedly in it. He returned the notepad to his shirt pocket and said, "I'm obliged. You've been a big help."

The little man smiled, "Don't mention it. Glad to oblige th' law."

Morgan left the telegraph office and walked to City Hall. He noticed that Rideout, who was leaning on a post at the sheriff's office, was watching him. He thought, "This ought to give 'em somethin' to think about."

Morgan stepped to the counter and said to the clerk, "I wanna see your deed ledgers."

"Can't do it," he said.

"Why not?"

"Just can't. Th' mayor an' city council have a policy that—" Morgan moved quickly behind the counter and started pulling the ledgers from the shelf. The clerk stammered, "Now see here! You can't—"

"I can't do what?" interrupted Morgan as he started leafing through the ledgers.

"I'm gonna go get th' sheriff," he sputtered.

Morgan never looked up, "You do that."

The clerk stared at Morgan for several moments and quickly left. Morgan found the ledger that contained the recent land transactions. He took out his notepad and copied down the names of the recent buyers and sellers. As Morgan opened the door to leave, the clerk returned.

"Th' sheriff wants to see you." He had a wry smile on his face, and his voice was smug.

"Is that a fact?" replied Morgan. He started toward the general store.

The clerk called after him, "Right now, he said." His voice trailed away as he thought, "He ain't th' least bit afraid of Luther. I wonder what he was lookin' for?"

Linda Farquar had her back to the door when Morgan entered. She said pleasantly, "I'll be with you in a minute—" She turned to the door, saw Morgan, and stopped in mid-sentence.

Morgan walked to the counter and said, "Mornin'. I was wonderin' if we might talk?"

"About horses?"

Morgan saw that she was trying to suppress a smile. "No, guns and ammunition." He had a wry smile on his lips; his eyes were alive.

Linda's faint smile turned into a frown. "Guns and ammunition?"

Morgan placed the Sharps cartridge casing from Walsh's murder site on the counter. "Have you had any call for Sharps cartridges of late?"

Linda picked up the casing, looked it over, and replied, "Not lately. Not much call for them anymore...since the buffalo..." She thought for a moment then continued, "Funny you should ask...a hunter came through here, I think it was in February or March. He wanted a box of Sharps." She turned and took a box of shells from the shelf and handed it to Morgan. I only had two boxes." She nodded to the box and added, "Go ahead and open it."

Morgan opened the box and said, "There're three cartridges missin'."

"The hunter noticed it right off also. I sold him the other box."

Morgan was thinking, "February or March...that was after Walsh was killed."

"Any idea about th' three missin' cartridges?"

Linda shook her head, "No, but I know both boxes were full at one time..." She stared quizzically at Morgan and asked, "What's this all about?"

"I'm not sure...probably nothin' to bother about." He thought for a moment and asked, "Do you know of anybody in Dog Bark who owns a Sharps?"

"I only know of one," she replied. Linda raised her eyebrows and continued, "Me. It was my dad's."

"May I see it?" he casually asked.

"I'll get it." She returned from the back room and placed the big rifle on the counter. "As far as I know, it hasn't been fired in years."

Morgan examined the rifle, thinking, "It's been too long to tell for sure, but I've got a hunch this is th' Sharps that was used to kill Walsh. Three missing cartridges? I wonder. I've got a feelin' in my gut…it's right here in front of me."

Morgan handed Linda the rifle. "Thanks." He gave her a list of supplies he needed and smiled, "County."

Linda took the list smiling, "There's been a lot of talk about you."

"Any of it good?" Morgan asked.

Linda began gathering the items on Morgan's list, and replied, "Most of it, but not all of it."

Morgan grinned, "Do you believe everything you've heard about me?"

She placed his supplies on the counter and replied, "I haven't made up my mind yet. But I do know one thing."

Morgan signed for his supplies and asked, "What's that?"

"That story you told about having to shoot that horse is pure bull." Her eyes were dancing.

"Saw through it right away, did ya?" grinned Morgan. He touched his hat, "Be seein' ya." He turned as he reached the door and said, "Th' last time we talked, you said you weren't sure whether you liked me or not…" His voice trailed off.

"I'm still not sure. I'll let you know when I make up my mind." Her voice and body language told Morgan otherwise.

Morgan closed the door, thinking, "That's a woman worth fightin' for. Maybe after this is over…" Myles Witherspoon and Doc O'Banion walked up and interrupted Morgan's thoughts.

"We were beginning to worry about you," said Doc.

Morgan shook their hands, "Worry?"

"Yeah, we heard about your run-in with those two yahoos at Blackthorn," Witherspoon said.

"No need to worry; wasn't much to it." Morgan's tone turned serious as he inquired, "Who'd you hear about it from?"

Doc looked at Witherspoon, Witherspoon looked at Doc; O'Banion answered, "I believe Phil Browne, the bartender at the One-Eyed Jack, was telling everyone about it yesterday."

Morgan sighed, "Like I said, Dog Bark has a big ear."

O'Banion chuckled, "Make an Indian elephant jealous."

Morgan laughed, "Nice seein' y'all again. I gotta get on th' trail to Blackthorn."

Witherspoon lowered his voice to a whisper and asked, "Is that fuse a long one or a short one?"

Morgan's face stiffened, and his eyes got darker, "It's shorter than it was th' last time we spoke, but, like I said, I'll let you know before I light it."

O'Banion and Witherspoon watched Morgan walk away. "Texas Ranger?" asked Doc.

"Could be, could be," replied Witherspoon. He scratched his chin and added, "I know one thing. He's here for a reason. I don't believe for a moment he just showed up looking for a deputy job. He's a cut above that."

"I agree," said Doc. "Myles, have you ever seen eyes like his? Gives you the willies, even if you haven't done anything wrong. I'd hate for him to be looking for me."

"Myself," said Witherspoon.

Morgan led Ebon out of his stall just as Tim came in. "Mornin', Mr. Morgan. I hope it was all right. I gave your horse some oats." Before Morgan could reply, Tim added, "Everybody's sayin' you killed two cowboys dead over at Blackthorn. Were they fast? Did you—"

"Whoa…hold on a minute, Tim. First of all, I didn't kill anybody. I just ran 'em outta town, and, yes, it was all right to give Ebon some oats." Morgan saw disappointment appear in Tim's eyes and on his face. He changed the subject, "How's Gunsight?"

"He's fine," smiled Tim. His smile faded, and he added, "I'm only feedin' him every other day."

"Atta boy…you're doin' right." Morgan mounted Ebon and asked, "Tim, has anybody come for their horse this mornin'?"

"Only Tiny…I mean Deputy Leatherwood. He left 'bout thirty minutes ago."

"Did he happen to say where he was goin'?"

"I heard him tell Pa he was goin' to Fort Griffin. Mr. Morgan, he was cussin' somethin' awful. Boy, he was sure 'nough mad at somebody."

Morgan flipped Tim a nickel, "I'm obliged. Get yourself a candy." He turned Ebon toward the door and called back, "Take care of Gunsight."

Tim ran out of the livery and called to Morgan. "Thanks, Mr. Morgan. Next time I'll brush your horse and…" He watched Morgan until he could no longer see him, then said, "Show you Gunsight."

Chapter Seventeen

Morgan left Dog Bark knowing that the need for secrecy was over; he knew that they knew that he knew, and he didn't care. He mused, "Ebon, it was just a matter of time; besides, it suits me this way. Th' best way to deal with varmints is to meet 'em head on. You gotta think like 'em…" Morgan rode for several moments deep in thought before he added, "And sometimes you gotta act like 'em."

Morgan went to his hiding place and picked up his U.S. Marshall badge, letter of appointment, and his and McEachern's notes. He headed for Blackthorn, riding a meandering route well off to the west of the main trail. His plan was to come into Blackthorn from the south, spend an hour or two there, then check the graveyard to see if McEachern and Coldiron had left a message. Morgan was in no hurry, and he stopped often to check his backtrail. He halted in a dry creek bed surrounded by cedars and brush.

Morgan drank from his canteen, thinking, "If Coldiron and McEachern find out what I'm thinkin' they'll find…all that's left is to find out who did th' killin'." He screwed on the cap and mused, "Leatherwood's my best bet…faced with th' moment of truth to save his hide. I've a feelin' he'll sell 'em out." Morgan tied the canteen to his saddle horn and thought, "Only one missing piece. Where's Jubal Carver? Can't shake th' feelin' he's still here. I feel it in my bones, and I ain't usually wrong."

Morgan rode into Blackthorn just as a thunderstorm hit. He left Ebon at the livery, donned his slicker, and walked to the saloon, thinking, "Leatherwood has had time to make Griffin. He's most likely on his way back…I wonder if he'll stop here? I hope so."

As was his custom, Morgan released the thong from the hammer of his Colt and entered the saloon. He took off his slicker and hung it on the coat rack by the door, all the while scanning the room. "I only see two…that's th' foreman of th' Kiowa Lance, Adcock…I don't know th' other one."

Morgan stepped to the bar, nodded to the two cowboys. "Howdy. It's gettin' a little rough out there."

"You can say that again," replied Adcock. "We just beat it ourselves. Come have a drink with us."

"Thanks. A drink sounds good." He went to their table and seated himself with his back to the wall.

"This here's Toby Smith," said Adcock.

Morgan stuck out his hand, "Stuart Morgan."

Smith shook Morgan's hand. "I've heard a lot about you."

Morgan smiled faintly, "Y'all didn't happen to see Leatherwood while you were at Griffin, did you?"

Adcock frowned slightly, "As a matter of fact we did. He was headed back to Dog Bark when we came in from th' Kiowa Lance. Why do you ask?"

"Nothin' in particular. I just need to palaver with him." Morgan looked around the saloon and asked, "Is Treywick around?"

Smith nodded his head toward the door. "He went down th' street for somethin'; said he'd be right back."

Morgan nodded his head and said to Adcock, "Roy, I'd like to ask a favor of you."

Adcock sat down his beer mug, eyed Morgan for a moment, then casually said, "Ask away."

"Try and convince Killpatrick to sit tight for a few more days. Tell him I've about got a handle on things."

Adcock studied Morgan for a moment before saying, "I'll tell him, but I can't promise you he'll do it. Jedd's fed up. He's gonna want to know details."

"He's just gonna hafta trust me." Morgan's voice was somber as he continued, "Now's not th' time for me to lay all my cards on th' table."

Adcock studied Morgan for several moments, then quietly said, "I'll do my best, but I ain't promisin' nothin'. Th' ol' man can be mighty stubborn."

Morgan smiled, "I'm obliged." He turned to Smith, "You were here th' night Chris Walsh disappeared, weren't you?"

"Yeah, I was. Played poker all night...why?"

Morgan didn't answer his question. "Did anybody leave th' game after Walsh left?"

Smith scratched his jaw, "Naw, not that I recollect."

"How about Treywick?"

Smith frowned and shook his head, "Naw, he was here th' whole time."

"Are you sure?"

"Yeah, I'm sure. What's this all about?"

Before Morgan could reply, Adcock asked, "Have you found out what happened to him?"

Morgan lied, "Not yet, but I'm workin' on it." He got up to leave and added, "Roy, is there someone at th' Circle H you can talk to?"

Adcock thought for a moment and said, "Dub Little and I were friends at one time…before all of this. I suppose I could try to talk with him."

Morgan put on his hat. "Ask him to talk to Haggard. Tell him to give me some time."

"I'll get it done," replied Adcock. "Any idea when you're gonna get to th' bottom of all this?"

"If things go like I think, three, four days; maybe a week. I gotta move. Be seein' ya." Morgan walked away, then stopped and said, "One more thing, Roy. I think it's best we keep this conversation between th' three of us and Killpatrick." When he saw Adcock's eyebrows raise, Morgan added, "I've reason to believe that you've got a fox in your henhouse—"

"All right," said Adcock. "You watch your back, hear?"

"I always do," Morgan replied.

After Morgan left, Smith asked, "What do you make of him?"

"I get th' feelin' he's a straight shooter. I like him." Adcock drummed his fingers on the table and added, "I know one thing. He's trouble for someone, and I'm glad he's not after me."

"He said we had a fox. Wonder who he's talkin' about?" asked Smith.

"That's a good question. It's kinda funny. I've been thinkin' along those same lines. A bunch of things don't add up lately." Adcock continued to drum his fingers on the table for a while before continuing, "I just might know a way of findin' out. If th' chickens are made available, maybe that fox just might get careless—"

Morgan came out of the livery just as the rain stopped. He spotted Treywick, who was headed back to the saloon; he rode up to him and asked, "Did Leatherwood come through here?"

Treywick wiped rain from his eyes. "Yeah, 'bout an hour ago. He—" Morgan rode off before Treywick finished. Treywick watched Morgan for a moment, then mused, "Well, howdy to you, too. I wuz gonna tell ya he wuz lookin' fer ya."

Morgan rode past the cemetery, then doubled back and waited under a big oak tree, which stood just outside the cemetery fence. While he waited, he scanned the area with his field glasses, but he saw nothing to arouse his suspicion of being watched. Morgan put away the field glasses, thinking, "Don't matter much anymore…I won't be needin' to use this place anymore. Now, if McEachern and Coldiron have got my information—"

Morgan dismounted and went to his hiding place; he rolled the rock over and mused, "Looks like my luck is holdin'." There were two messages, one each from McEachern and Coldiron. Morgan read the messages, then put them in his pocket, thinking, "Now it all makes sense. All of 'em are originally from Missouri and Kansas. McEachern said most of 'em rode with Quantrell—Jayhawkers during and after th' war. McEachern's gonna be in Fort Worth 'til next Saturday. Damn. I was countin' on him bein'…" Morgan's mind raced through many possibilities before he decided, "I ain't waitin' on him. Maybe Dobby, Adcock or Chacon will help, if I need someone."

Morgan pulled out Coldiron's message, read it again, and thought, "I knew there had to be some mighty big stakes for them to risk killin' all those men. The only thing left is to find out who did th' killin', and I aim to do just that."

Morgan climbed on Ebon and said, "Ebon, I'm gonna give you that double ration of oats anyway." Morgan patted Ebon on the neck and chuckled, "You did take that bet, didn't you?"

Morgan rode on the east side of the main trail to Dog Bark. His thoughts bounced back and forth from McEachern's and Coldiron's messages to Tiny Leatherwood. He stopped to take a swig from his canteen. "McEachern said he had no information on Treywick or Crow. Th' new information on Jubal Carver ain't much help, or is it? And Crow?" Morgan retrieved Coldiron's message and reread it. As he read it again, a smile came to his face. "I must be gettin' old, Ebon. I almost missed that one."

Morgan put away the message, feeling as though a mountain had been lifted from his back. "After all these years, maybe he's made a mistake, and I'm gonna be there to point it out to him. Damn straight."

Morgan's thoughts returned to Leatherwood. "Treywick said he'd just came through Blackthorn. I wonder if he's up ahead waitin' for me? I've got a notion he is. Maybe in th' same spot used to bushwhack Walsh." Morgan checked his Colt, Winchester, and the Sharps. He loaded the Sharps, then rode a wide path that would allow him to come up behind the place where he thought Leatherwood would be.

Morgan left Ebon in a grove of cottonwood trees and moved quietly down the hill, taking his Winchester and field glasses. He stopped some five hundred yards from the trail below and took out his glasses; he found the familiar spot, and what he saw made him say, "Tiny, I knew you wouldn't disappoint me, you backshootin' coward."

Leatherwood was talking softly to himself as Morgan slipped quietly up behind him. Morgan moved in closer and heard Tiny whisper, "Just one clean shot. All I'm askin' for…just one…" He swallowed his thoughts when he heard Morgan's calm voice close behind him.

"One move and I'll kill ya."

Leatherwood began to tremble as he stammered, "Where'd you come from?" He propped his rifle against a boulder, slowly raised his hands, and turned to face Morgan. His eyes were wide, and he was visibly shaking.

Morgan cocked his pistol. "Doin' a little huntin'?"

Leatherwood said with a crooked grin, "As a matter of fact I am...I saw a buck with a big—"

Morgan cut him off, "I ain't in no mood, Tiny. I want some answers, and I want 'em fast. Who shot Chris Walsh?"

Tiny licked his lips. "I wouldn't know. Even if I did, I wouldn't tell you." He moved his hands and slowly unfastened the buckle to his gun belt and holster. As it hit the ground he smugly said, "I know your kind, Morgan. You ain't got th' stomach to shoot an unarmed man." Leatherwood moved slowly toward Morgan.

A look of disbelief jumped into Tiny's eyes when Morgan shot him in the right kneecap. He fell with a thud and cried, "My leg! You son of a bitch! Goddamn you, Morgan."

Morgan watched, showing no emotion as Leatherwood managed to stand up and begin moving once again toward him, hopping on his left leg. Leatherwood snarled, "I'm gonna kill you if it's th' last—"

Morgan's Colt bellowed again; the slug slammed into Tiny's left ankle, once again knocking the big man down.

Leatherwood rolled over, cursing, "O shit. Goddamn that hurts. Damn you Morgan, I shoulda killed you that first day."

Morgan stepped to Tiny and kicked him in the face. "That first one was for Chris Walsh." Leatherwood rolled over and managed to get on all fours. Morgan kicked him again. "Th' second one was for Harvey Pickett." He kicked him again and added, "And these are for Gill Warner."

Leatherwood's face was a bloody mess. He was groaning but cursing profusely. Morgan stood back and watched stoically as Leatherwood managed to sit up. He squatted down in front of him and casually said, "You got two options. You either tell me what I wanna know, or..." Morgan reached out and grabbed Tiny by the shirt collar and shook him violently, then continued, "Or I'm gonna leave you out here for th' wolves and coyotes, like y'all left Walsh."

Morgan backhanded Tiny across the face and added, "You hear me?"

"Yeah, I hear you," he groaned. "You can go to hell. I ain't got nothin' to say."

"Well, suit yourself." Morgan stood up and walked away as Leatherwood began crawling toward his gun belt.

Morgan let him get within a foot of the pistol, then moved swiftly to him and stomped his right wrist with his boot. Morgan heard the bone break and said, "I told you I didn't fight fair."

Leatherwood rolled over onto his back, muttering through clenched teeth, "Fuck you, Morgan! Damn, th' pain is killin' me!" He rolled his head and eyes to Morgan and whispered, "Damn you. Finish me…finish me."

Morgan gathered up Tiny's pistol and rifle and said, "I'm gonna get my horse. When I get back, I'm gonna ask you for th' last time. If you don't come up with some right answers, I'm gonna leave you here as buzzard bait. You be thinkin' 'bout that." Morgan climbed on Leatherwood's horse and rode back to get Ebon.

Morgan returned to find Leatherwood unmoving just where he left him. Morgan dismounted, thinking, "Maybe he's dead. It don't much matter to me one way or th' other."

As Morgan approached, Leatherwood opened his eyes, sat up, and weakly said, "If I tell ya, what's in it for me?"

Morgan squatted down beside him. "If you come clean, I'll take you to the doc in Fort Griffin."

Leatherwood closed his eyes and whispered, "What do you wanna know?"

Although he already knew the answers, Morgan wanted confirmation from Leatherwood.

Morgan asked, "Who's in this with you?"

Tiny licked at a trickle of blood running from the corner of his mouth and mumbled, "Luther and Rideout and..." He hesitated.

Morgan waited for a moment, then said, "Tiny, I told you I ain't in no mood for—"

"Burkett and Zachary and...and..." Leatherwood coughed up blood and again closed his eyes.

Morgan grabbed Tiny by the ears and shook his head, "And who else, Tiny?"

Tiny opened his eyes and whispered, "Wesley...Wesley Jones. Yeah, Wesley."

Morgan twisted his ears. "You're forgettin' someone, aren't you?"

Leatherwood winced, "Yeah, I 'most forgot...Collins. Yeah, Collins."

Morgan pondered what Leatherwood had said, then asked, "Who's playin' th' Indian?"

Leatherwood pawed at his mouth with his left hand and mumbled, "Collins."

Morgan thought to himself, "I thought so."

"You're doin' fine. A few more questions, and I'll get you to th' Doc. Where's Jubal Carver?"

Leatherwood batted his eyes and grimaced, "I don't know no Jubal Carver."

Morgan pressed his foot on Tiny's shattered knee. "Wrong answer, Tiny."

Tiny clawed at his leg, "O sweet Jesus, that hurts. Goddamn, Morgan, I'm tellin' it straight."

Morgan removed his foot and thought for a moment, then said, "Who set Ned Farkle on me?"

"Honest to God, Morgan. I don't know. It wasn't us."

Morgan went to Ebon, got his canteen and returned to Leatherwood; he squatted in front of Tiny and took a long pull from the canteen.

Leatherwood ran his swollen tongue over his teeth and lips. "Gimme a drink, and I'll tell you anything you wanna know."

Morgan screwed the cap back on. "After you tell me."

Leatherwood stared at Morgan with blank eyes. "Morgan, you're a real hard-ass, ain't you?"

"It's been said of me," replied Morgan. His voice was flat. "Who was in on th' robbery of th' army payroll?"

"Me, Rideout, Zachary, an' Collins."

"Who did th' killin'?"

"Collins killed Pickett," he whispered. "Shot him with a bow an' arrow."

"And Gill Warner?"

Leatherwood began to shake as he said, "Rideout…and…" His voice faded away.

Morgan finished his sentence. "And you."

Leatherwood didn't reply. Morgan slapped his face. "Who pulled th' trigger?"

Tiny cursed, "Goddamnit, it was me. Are you happy?"

Morgan slapped him hard. "No, Tiny, I ain't happy. Ain't gonna be 'til you and them other bushwhackers are in hell." Morgan's voice got harder and his eyes darker as he continued, "Who killed Chris Walsh?"

Leatherwood managed a faint smile, "I know you ain't gonna believe me." He grimaced in pain and continued, "But at this point I don't giv'a shit one way or th' other." He looked at Morgan for a moment, then said evenly, "I didn't even know he was dead 'til you mentioned it."

Morgan studied Leatherwood for a moment, stood up, and casually said, "I believe you, Tiny." He squatted down again and put his face just inches from Tiny's. "I think there's a bunch of things they didn't tell you…like they were plannin' on killin' you as soon as you were of no more use to 'em.

They've played you for th' fool that you are."

Morgan took the cap from the canteen and gave the canteen to Tiny, who took it quickly with his left hand and drank lustily. Morgan let him drink his fill before taking the canteen from him. Leatherwood wiped his mouth and said, "Ain't nobody ever played Tiny Leatherwood for a fool...and lived to tell about it."

"They ain't?" laughed Morgan. "Let me guess. They promised you a piece of th' Circle H after y'all ran Haggard off, right?"

"Hell no, th' Kiowa Lance. A big piece. They—"

Morgan interrupted, "I guess they forgot to tell you there wasn't gonna be a Kiowa Lance or Circle H when they got what they wanted."

Leatherwood had a puzzled look on his face as he said, "No Kiowa...Circle Lance...they wouldn't—"

"They would, and they did," deadpanned Morgan. "It's my guess they're gonna kill Rideout, Zachary, and Jones when they are no longer of any use to 'em."

The information Morgan was giving Leatherwood, coupled with the pain and shock that he was feeling, had Tiny confused. "Jack? Me and him are...you said they? Who? Why? Who in th' hell is they?"

Morgan sighed, "Tiny, you're thicker'n I first thought. Piper, Burkett, Collins, and Jubal Carver are th' chiefs. Th' rest of y'all are just little'ns."

Leatherwood opened his mouth to speak just as the crack of a gunshot sounded; the bullet slammed into his head and killed him instantly. The second shot rang out as Morgan dove towards the rocks; he felt a hot sting in the fingers of his right hand. Morgan Indian-crawled to the rocks, thinking, "That'll be Collins or Rideout."

He looked at his hand and saw that the bullet passed between his little and index fingers, tearing a small piece of flesh from each. He shook his hand and thought, "I don't think th' bones are broken…piece of luck there."

Morgan peeked over the rock just as a horse and rider came running out of the brush and started up the trail to Dog Bark. Morgan sprinted to Ebon and got his Sharps rifle, thinking, "He's still only three hundred yards away…got plenty of time." He quickly adjusted the sights of the big rifle and took dead aim. When the horse and rider reached the top of the grade on the trail, Morgan fired. The sound of the big rifle was still echoing when Morgan saw the rider lurch forward as the big slug hit him. Three strides later, the rider slid off the horse to the ground.

Morgan moved to the lifeless body of Leatherwood and said, "Tiny, I said that first day I was gonna hafta kill ya. I was wrong. One of your friends beat me to it."

Chapter Eighteen

Morgan wrapped his hand with his bandanna and went to see who he'd shot. He stopped well short of the fallen man, thinking, "Careful, Morgan, you've already made one mistake." He studied the body through his field glasses for a moment and mused, "Can't tell who it is, but he's sure as hell dead."

Morgan palmed his Colt with his left hand and slowly rode to the prone body. The first thing he noticed was the man was wearing moccasins. Morgan dismounted and moved to the dry-gulcher. When he was near, he said, "Mr. Collins, your days of bushwhackin' and playin' Indian are over."

Morgan's thoughts were rushing through his head. He

now knew that he was going to have to move fast; he climbed back on Ebon and headed for Blackthorn. "Ebon, give me all you got. All hell's fixin' to break loose." By the time Morgan reached Blackthorn, he had formulated his plan. He was relieved to see Adcock, and Smith's horses were still in front of the saloon. He stuck his extra Colt in his belt and went into the saloon.

Once inside, he walked quickly to the two cowboy's table and said, "Boys, things are startin' to pop. I need your help, and I need it now."

Adcock looked at Morgan's bloody hand. "What th' hell's happened? Are you hurt bad?"

"It's just a scratch." Morgan quickly told them what had happened. He finished by saying, "Here's what I need." He took out his note pad and pencil and began writing. "Toby, can you take Leatherwood and Collins to Fort Griffin for me?"

Smith nodded his head, "Sure thing."

Treywick, who had been listening, said as he was leaving, "I'll get Pedro to give ya a hand."

Morgan finished writing and gave the note to Smith. "Give this to Sheriff Dobby." He began writing again and said to Adcock, "Roy, Zachary's gonna light out soon as he hears about Tiny and Collins. I want you to be sure he don't skedaddle on us."

A wry smile appeared on Adcock's face. "He our fox?"

"Uh-huh. He and Jones at th' Circle H have been workin' both sides of th' fence."

"Why, that sorry bastard," growled Smith. "I thought he smelled. We oughta—"

"I need him alive," interrupted Morgan. His eyes turned pitch black as he added, "He might be th' only one of 'em that's still able to talk…come this time tomorrow."

Morgan finished his second note and gave it to Smith. "Send this wire to United States Marshall Wallace McEachern as soon as you get to Griffin."

Smith put the message in his pocket. "I best get movin' if I want to get to Fort Griffin before dark."

After Smith left, Adcock asked, "Just for th' record, who're you workin' for?"

Morgan unpinned his deputy badge and replaced it with his U.S. Marshall badge. "Roy, has anybody been offerin' to buy th' Kiowa Lance lately?"

"As a matter of fact, they have, several times."

"Who's doin' th' offerin'?"

"Killpatrick told me Freeman Burkett made th' offer. He told th' ol' man he was negotiatin' for some gent back east. If it's any help to you, I hear he's offered to buy th' Circle H, too."

Morgan thought for a moment before saying, "Roy, you'd better get movin'. I don't want any of these snakes to slither off on me. I'll fill you in on all th' details th' next time I see you."

Adcock stood up and asked, "What about Jones?"

"I'll take care of him. You just be sure and take Zachary outta th' picture."

"All right. I was just thinkin'; you're gonna have your hands full with Piper and Rideout...and Burkett. Th' ol' man is gonna want to help when I tell him—"

"I appreciate it, but this is my fight. I'll handle it."

Adcock studied Morgan for a moment, then nodded his head, "Suit yourself. I'll bring Zachary to Dog Bark when you get word to me. Good luck to you. Be seein' ya."

Morgan smiled, "You too, Roy. I'm obliged."

Treywick returned and said, "Damn. You killed both of 'em. What'd they do, throw down on you?"

Morgan gave Treywick ten dollars and casually said, "Somethin' like that. Here's th' money Tiny owed you."

Morgan pushed Ebon hard on the way to Dog Bark; he wanted to get some sleep and have O'Banion take a look at his fingers. He saw the glow of lights up ahead and mused, "Ebon, I'm gonna have to be at my best tomorrow…gotta get some sleep." He gently shook his right hand and added, "Looks like all my practicin' with th' left hand is gonna pay off…I hope."

Morgan left Ebon in a stand of oak, elm, and cedar trees; he patted the gelding and soothed, "Sorry, ol' pard, but I can't let them know I'm in town. I'll be back for you come first light."

He took his two rifles, the extra Colt, and the left-handed belt and holster and started walking to Dog Bark, thinking, "I'm gonna take 'em tomorrow, left-handed if I have to. They may run for it if word about Leatherwood and Collins gets out. Only way for that to happen is for Treywick…" Morgan dismissed that thought and thought, "No, I don't think he will. They think they're in th' clear…maybe that an' th' element of surprise will give me th' edge."

Morgan made his way behind the stairs to O'Banion's office and was about to start up when he heard someone coming; he flattened himself against the wall and waited. When Morgan saw who it was, he whispered, "Miss Farquar, Stuart Morgan, over here."

Morgan's voice momentarily startled her, but, when she saw who it was, Linda moved quickly to him and whispered, "You've got to get out of sight. They're looking for you."

"Upstairs," Morgan quietly said. "I've got to see th' doc." They moved quickly up the stairs. Just as they reached the top, the door opened, and O'Banion stepped out. Morgan said, "Evenin', Doc. I lit that fuse. I've got some business for you."

O'Banion closed the door and pulled down the shade. "I was beginning to worry about you. Piper and Rideout are looking for you. They're telling everybody you murdered Ned Farkle."

"So that's their game," chuckled Morgan. He began to unwrap his hand. "Have a look, Doc. It's startin' to trouble me a mite."

O'Banion put on his glasses, examined Morgan's hand, and remarked, "Gunshot, right?"

"Gunshot!" said Linda. "You've been shot?"

"It's just a scratch," Morgan said. "I've had worse."

"Maybe so," said O'Banion. "But, sometimes these little ones turn into big ones. It's a good thing you came to me. It's infected." He looked at Morgan's badge and chuckled, "U. S. Marshal, huh? I figured as much."

While O'Banion treated and wrapped his hand, Morgan told them about Leatherwood and Collins. He finished by saying, "There's a lot more to it...I ain't got th' time to tell ya all th' details. That'll hafta wait 'til this is all over."

Morgan unbuckled his belt and holster and replaced it with the left-handed rig. "You can't fight them...they'll...you're hurt," stammered Linda.

Morgan tied the holster to his leg. "I'll make do. This is my job, my fight."

"She's right," said O'Banion. "You've got to get help. Maybe—"

Morgan interrupted, "Y'all can help me by stayin' out of it. Been enough people hurt; 'sides, I've sent word to Sheriff Dobby over at Fort Griffin." He slipped his Colt into its holster and stuck the spare Colt into his belt, "Are they in town?"

"Rideout left for Hanging Tree about mid-afternoon," answered O'Banion. "I haven't seen Piper since early morning. Burkett's over at the One-Eyed Jack."

Morgan was thinking, "Piper sent Leatherwood north and Rideout south...box me in. Collins was probably on his way to Dog Bark when he heard th' shots. I'm guessin' he'll have Jones meet Rideout at Hangin' Tree. Adcock should have Zachary outta th' way by now. Piper's countin' on him and Burkett handlin' me here at Dog Bark. Maybe with some help from Jubal. Pretty clever of him comin' up with th' Farkle murder charge."

Morgan turned to Linda, "Could you rustle me up some grub?" He nodded toward the couch and asked O'Banion, "If it's all right with you, I need to get some shut eye. I'm goin' to Hangin' Tree come first light."

"But Jack's at Hanging Tree!" Linda exclaimed. "You're in no condition to…" Her voice faded as her face colored slightly. She quickly composed herself and added, "I'll get you something to eat."

As she started to the door, Morgan said quietly, "You be careful. They may be watchin'." Linda nodded her head and slipped quietly out the door.

O'Banion locked the door after her and said, "Rideout's mighty fast." He paused, pointed to Morgan's left hand. "Are you any…?" Before he could finish, Morgan's pistol appeared in his hand as if by magic. He holstered the Colt, and O'Banion said, "Yes, I guess you are."

Morgan flexed his right hand and said, "Doc, any chance of my hand gettin' better by tomorrow?"

"No," replied O'Banion. "If anything, it's going to be worse." He tugged at his ear and added, "I'm going to give you some medical advice." He smiled and continued, "That I know you aren't going to take." He studied Morgan for a moment, then sighed, "Oh, what th' hell…you've already made up your mind."

Morgan chuckled, "Thanks, Doc…and you're right…I have made up my mind. I can't take a chance of lettin' 'em get away; 'sides I made Chris Walsh a promise, and I aim to keep it, even if it kills me."

Morgan was on the move a good hour before sunrise; he ate the biscuits and jerky Linda had brought him, then went to the livery to get oats for Ebon. He noticed Rideout's sorrel was gone. After feeding and rubbing down Ebon, Morgan headed for Hanging Tree. After several minutes of riding, Morgan's right hand began to throb. "Doc was right. It's worse."

Morgan forced the thoughts of his injured hand from his mind and thought about his plan. "Odds are better takin' 'em one at a time. I hope Rideout is still at Hangin' Tree. Take some luck buckin' 'em all at th' same time, even with two good hands."

Morgan made Hangin' Tree by mid-morning, but waited until noon before riding in. He smiled when he saw Rideout's sorrel in front of the saloon; he checked both of his six-shooters and slowly rode to the saloon. He slid off Ebon and whispered, "Stand easy, boy. I won't be long." Morgan released the thong from the hammer of his Colt and went in.

Rideout was sitting at a table in the center of the room; at his left sat Wesley Jones. Morgan thought, "Good. At least I know where he is." He quickly scanned the room and saw that Mendoza was behind the bar. Rosa and Maria were at a table just to the right of Rideout and Jones. Two elderly Mexican men were standing at the bar. Rideout, Mendoza, and Jones were laughing as Morgan entered. When they saw Morgan, their laughter died. As soon as the two Mexicans saw Morgan, they downed their drinks and moved quickly by him and left.

Rideout stood up and grinned, "I was beginnin' to think you'd left th' county. Luther sent me and Tiny to fetch ya. Somethin's brewin' between Killpatrick and Haggard. Tiny just left to—"

"You're a liar," said Morgan.

The grin faded from Rideout's face. He moved away from the table and asked, "What'd you say?"

"You heard me," replied Morgan. He tossed Leatherwood's badge at Rideout's feet. "Tiny left all right...yesterday...for Hell."

Rideout noticed Morgan's bandaged hand for the first time; a wicked smile appeared on his lips as his eyes danced. "Y'all heard him. Called me a liar. He's callin' me out. It's gonna be a fair fight."

"I'm only gonna say this one time," warned Morgan. "I'm a United States Marshall. I'm arrestin' th' both of ya for th' murders of Gill Warner, Harvey Pickett, and U. S. Marshall Chris Walsh. You can unbuckle them gun belts or fill your hands." Morgan paused to let his revelation and challenge sink in. He then added, "It don't matter one way or th' other to me."

Jones stood up and stammered, "Murder! I ain't killed nobody. Sure, I started some fires…ran some cattle—"

"Wesley, shut your mouth," snapped Rideout. "He's dug his own grave. Ain't no way he can take th' two of us…looks like ol' Tiny got a lick or two in."

"No, that was your friend Collins," deadpanned Morgan. He smiled for the first time as his eyes turned dead-of-night dark. "He's joined Tiny in Hell."

The bat wings opened slowly, and Morgan heard Chacon say in Spanish as he moved to Morgan's side. "I will take señor Jones, friend."

Morgan answered, "Gracias." He then said to Rideout, "If you decide to pull that six-shooter, there's somethin' you should know."

"And what's that?" asked Rideout. His voice was thick with sarcasm.

"Same thing I told Tiny, right before he died. Piper, Burkett, and Jubal have played you for a fool."

Rideout frowned, "Jubal? I don't know no Jubal."

"Yeah, I know. You also don't know they were gonna kill ya', right before they sold all th' land to th' government."

Rideout's mouth flew open, and his eyes got big. "Government?"

"Uh-huh…Department of th' Interior…for a Comanche and Kiowa Indian reservation."

Rideout tried to talk but couldn't get his words out; he finally cleared his throat and growled, "A fool like Tiny might buy your bullshit, but…" Rideout's hand moved rattlesnake-quick to his pistol. As the barrel of Rideout's forty-four started up, Morgan's Colt roared. The forty-five slug caught Rideout in the throat and spun him around. He clutched at his throat with his left hand as his pistol dropped to the floor. Rideout staggered toward Mendoza and gurgled, "Damn. He's killed me." He pitched forward, already dead when he crashed head-first into the bar."

Morgan saw that Chacon had Jones covered. Wesley raised his hands. "Don't shoot. I didn't kill nobody. I wuz just followin' orders. They said they'd kill me if—"

"Wesley, shut up." Morgan's voice was flat. He walked to Rideout and rolled him over with the toe of his boot, thinking, "I ain't there yet; I aimed at his heart." Morgan picked up Farkle's Colt and said, "That's twice…" He stuck the pistol into his belt, then took Rideout's deputy badge and retrieved Leatherwood's badge.

"We couldn't warn you," said Rosa. "Jack said he'd kill us if—"

"It's all right, Rosa." Morgan turned to Mendoza and stared at him.

"Hell, Morgan…I couldn't…Rideout was gonna kill me if I let on. I—"

Morgan punched a cartridge into his Colt and said, "Mendoza, I've got some unfinished business at Dog Bark." He holstered his pistol and added, "Don't be here when I get back."

Mendoza's bottom lip was quivering as he whispered, "I ain't 'fraid of you…I was plannin' on goin' down to Concho anyways. If I wanted to, I'd stay."

"Suit yourself," replied Morgan. "But remember what I said." He stared at Mendoza until the Mexican turned away, then said to Chacon, "Amigo, I was sure glad to hear your voice. It was a real piece of luck, you showin' up."

Chacon smiled, "No, she no luck. Señor Haggard, he send

me for to get Señor Jones."

Jones whined, "Chacon, you tell Haggard I didn't—"

"Wesley, I told you to shut up," said Morgan. "I ain't gonna tell you again." After a moment of unnatural silence, Morgan spoke to Chacon in Spanish, "Take him over to th' Kiowa Lance. Tell Adcock to take him and Zachary to Fort Griffin." He switched to English, "If he gives you any trouble…" Morgan turned and looked at Jones and continued, "Shoot him."

Chacon grinned, "It will be as you say." He waved his gun at Jones, "Move, hombre." He said to Morgan in Spanish, "Rafael, he no forget that day. May God be with you. Adios, amigo."

Morgan went to Rideout and searched his pockets, finding twelve dollars; he gave the money to Rosa and Maria and said, "It ain't enough, but maybe it'll cover what Leatherwood owes you." He touched the brim of his hat. "Ladies."

After Morgan had gone, Rosa said in a voice that sounded as though it had gone long unused. "Maria, that is one helluva man. Where was he when I…" The quiet, quivery voice faded.

Chapter Nineteen

Morgan rode very slowly to Dog Bark for two reasons; he was in no real hurry, and he wanted Piper to wait and worry. He ate jerky and biscuits as he rode. Taking a sip from his canteen, he thought, "They more'n likely are thinking either Collins, Leatherwood, or Rideout got th' job done. If my luck holds, they ain't got word of Leatherwood and Collins…no way they could have heard 'bout Rideout."

A jackrabbit bounded across the trail, causing Morgan to muse, "Ebon, they may be on th' run." He rode on for a while, then said, "No, I don't think so. No reason for 'em to. They've come too far, got too much at stake." He patted Ebon's neck and continued, "Besides, if I know human nature, greed's gonna dictate their reasonin'. I feel it in my bones, Ebon. They're gonna stand and fight, and that suits me. Damn straight, it does."

It was fully dark when Morgan reached Dog Bark. He rode down the quiet, empty street to Willson's livery.

"It's quiet, mighty quiet." Morgan gave Ebon hay and oats, checked both of his pistols, and was on his way out when Kyle Willson slipped quietly in.

"Burkett's down at th' hotel, eatin'. Piper's over at th' One-Eyed Jack." Willson fumbled with his watch chain, finally retrieved his watch, and nervously added, "They've been there 'bout an hour. Just thought you'd like to know."

Morgan nodded his head. "I'm obliged, Kyle."

Burkett was so startled when he saw Morgan, he dropped his fork. The other three patrons quickly left. "You dropped your fork," said Morgan, casually.

Burkett, visibly shaken, stammered, "I didn't—"

Morgan didn't let him finish, "You didn't what?" When Burkett didn't answer immediately, Morgan added, "You were about to say you didn't expect to see me, ain't that right?"

Burkett said with a crooked grin, "No that ain't it at all. You just surprised me, that's all."

"Uh-huh." Morgan stared hard at Burkett for a moment, then quietly stated, "I'm a U. S. Marshall. You're under arrest for murder."

Burkett rolled his eyes and stuttered, "Murder?"

"Yeah, murder. You got two options. You can unbuckle that iron or use it."

Burkett got up slowly and began flexing the fingers of his right hand, all the while staring at Morgan. After several seconds of heavy silence, he unbuckled his gun. "I ain't killed nobody. I reckon I'll take my chances in court."

"We're goin' over to th' jail," Morgan said. "You make one false move, I'll kill ya. It's as simple as that."

After locking up Burkett, Morgan walked slowly to the One-Eyed Jack. Tossing the cell keys in the water trough, he palmed his Colt and walked in. He saw only three people: Piper, Phil Browne, and Joel Crow. Browne was cleaning glasses. Piper was staring at the door and Morgan. Crow was lying face down on his hands at a table in the back.

As soon as Browne saw Morgan, he dropped his glass and rag and started to leave.

"Plant yourself," Morgan ordered.

Browne laughed nervously, "I wuz jus' gonna—"

"Do what I told you," warned Morgan.

Browne grinned crazily, "All right."

"I'll take that badge," said Piper. "You're under arrest for th' murder of Ned Farkle."

"Is that a fact?"

"Yeah, it's a fact all right. I've got an eye witness." He moved away from the bar and continued, "I'm hoping you'll come peaceable."

"I just bet you are." Morgan cocked his Colt. "Luther, I'm a United States Marshall. You're under arrest for the murders of Marshall Chris Walsh, Harvey Pickett, and Gill Warner."

Piper saw Morgan's badge for the first time, and his jaw dropped. He was at loss for words for several moments, but finally hissed, "U.S. Marshall, huh?" He licked his lips and smiled crookedly, "I figured as much, but it don't matter."

"It don't, huh?" Morgan saw that Piper didn't seem too worried. Morgan chuckled to himself because he knew why Piper felt so confident.

"No, it don't," laughed Piper. He pointed to the door behind Morgan. "Jack and Tiny are fixin' to blow your brains out." He laughed again, "Whadaya think about that?"

Morgan had his, Tiny's, and Rideout's badges in his right hand; he tossed them at Piper's feet and said casually, "If they're behind me, I think it's a real short trip to hell and back."

Piper stared at the badges for a long time. There wasn't a sound to be heard. Morgan could sense that, for the first time, Piper was beginning to have some doubt about his plans.

Morgan broke the silence. "Don't bother countin' on th' others, either." Apprehension appeared in Piper's eyes as Morgan continued in a laconic voice, "Your Indian, Collins, has got dirt in his face. Those other three weasels, Burkett, Zachary, and Jones…" Morgan nodded his head and raised one eyebrow, "Well, let's just say you can't count on 'em."

"But you can count on us," came a voice just outside. Morgan recognized Witherspoon's voice; the bat-wings opened and Witherspoon and O'Banion stepped in. O'Banion held a Winchester rifle; Witherspoon was carrying a double-barreled shotgun.

Witherspoon pointed the shotgun at Piper and winked at Morgan. "We wanted to be here when you lit that fuse."

Morgan moved to Piper and took his pistol, then tossed it to O'Banion. "I'm obliged. I'd appreciate it if y'all'd take this piece of puke over to th' jail." He pushed Piper toward them. "Th' keys are in th' trough out front."

"It's a pleasure," chuckled Witherspoon. He waved the shotgun at the door. "Get a move-on, sheriff. I hope I don't get nervous. This shotgun's got a hair-trigger."

"So has this rifle," chortled O'Banion. He turned to Morgan. "Are you coming?"

Morgan was staring at Crow. "I'll be along." He nodded his head to Browne. "Join 'em." After they had gone, Morgan holstered his Colt and moved closer to Crow, who hadn't moved since Morgan entered the saloon. Morgan took the four double eagle gold pieces he had taken from Ned Farkle, and threw them on the table. Crow didn't move.

"Jubal, you get what you pay for. You didn't get your money's worth in Ned, Jim Bob, or Catfish." Morgan's quiet voice sounded sharp and hard. Jubal Carver moved for the first time. He slowly raised his head; he wore a wry smile on his face. "Your little game is over," continued Morgan. He took one step back and added, "Now you get up an' get yours."

Jubal got up slowly, still smiling. He moved his arms away from his body and said, "Well now! Aren't you th' clever one."

The sight and memory of his father lying dead flashed through Morgan's mind and turned his eyes pitch black and his voice cold and hard; every fiber in his body told him to kill Jubal Carver. He then heard McEachern's voice, "Let th' law hang him…then his own…it'll be his option."

"You're under arrest…for murder," Morgan said evenly. He was watching Jubal's eyes, thinking, "His eyes will tell me when."

Jubal moved away from the table. "Murder?" He slowly lowered his arms. "Mind tellin' me who?"

"Chris Walsh and Henry Morgan." Morgan spread his legs slightly and continued. "You've got two options. Drop that gun, or use it."

"Oh, I'm gonna use it all right," he laughed. "But after all these years, what's a few more minutes? Morgan, you've got blood in your eyes." He chuckled and continued, "Can't say as I blame you." He eyed Morgan for a moment and said, "It ain't gonna matter none, but I didn't mean to kill your ol' man…first man I ever killed. It troubled me some for the longest while."

"But not enough to quit killin'?"

The smile faded from Jubal's face. "From what I hear, you oughtta know more 'bout that than me."

"I ain't never killed a man that didn't need killin'." He thought, "'Cept th' Kiowa brave."

"That's where me and you differ. I guess you're gonna tell me you didn't mean to kill Chris Walsh."

Jubal smiled, "Naw, I ain't. I meant to kill him all right,

and all the others, too." His smile thinned, then faded. "Mind tellin' me how you figured it out?"

"Like you said, what's a few more minutes? Even murderin' trash like you should know, before they meet their maker."

"Save th' sermon," said Jubal. "There ain't nothin' after this," his voice becoming harsher with each word.

Morgan warmed inside as he saw Jubal begin to lose his composure. "Pretty clever posin' as th' town drunk. Had me fooled for a while, 'til you gave yourself away."

"Gave myself away?" The tone of his voice said he didn't believe it.

"Uh-huh. Th' night I saw you pour out th' bottle of whiskey. Drunks don't pour out whiskey. They'll do a lot of things, but pourin' out whiskey ain't one of 'em. Got me to thinkin', and I did some checkin'." Morgan paused and stared knowingly at Jubal. He knew he had Jubal's curiosity aroused, and he was going to make him wonder and sweat for a while longer.

"Checkin'?" snapped Jubal.

"Yep, I did. Jubal, you'd be surprised what you can find out about a feller, if you know where to look. Now you take th' telegraph office; th' clerk keeps good records. You got a wire from Karl Woodson th' day before I left Fort Worth." The look in Jubal's eyes told Morgan that he had guessed right.

He continued, all the while staring into Jubal's eyes, "Your mother's maiden name was Crow; she had a brother. Seems this brother had a position with th' Department of th' Interior…" Morgan smiled as Jubal's jaw dropped.

Morgan's eyes turned even darker as he whispered, "Jubal, what's your uncle's name?" Jubal stood staring at Morgan, his mind a jumble of racing, fragmented thoughts. Before he could answer, Morgan said quietly, "Joel Crow, and in case you wanna know, he ain't workin' there no more. There ain't gonna be no land deal. Th' reservation is gonna stay at Fort Sill."

Jubal finally managed to speak. "I told Piper you weren't like th' others," he muttered. "But, no, he wouldn't listen. I shoulda killed you that first day in th' livery." He thought for a moment and added, "Maybe it still ain't too late." He licked his lips and grinned. "But I need to know how you knew I was th' one who shot Walsh. Tiny and Jack couldn't have told you; they didn't even know I was runnin' th' show, or who I was."

"That was th' easy part. Before they died, they said they didn't kill Walsh, didn't know who did, didn't know who you were. They also didn't know about th' Indian reservation y'all were workin' on. I believed them." Morgan nodded his head, "Collins and Zachary were at th' poker game. It had to be you."

"I think you made a lucky guess. It could have been Piper."

"You think what you wanna think." Morgan's voice was cool and casual.

"Well, it could have," spat Jubal. He moved a step to his right and added, "What if it was him…and I lied…it wasn't me?"

Morgan moved a step to his left. "Oh, it was you all right. You're th' only one who had easy access to Linda Farquar's Sharps…bein' as you swept out th' store. You didn't think anyone'd ever notice th' three missin' cartridges, did ya?" Morgan watched quietly as Jubal thought about what he'd just told him. He then said, "I found Walsh where you left him. The wolves and coyotes got at him." Morgan's tone was threatening the same savage violence as the animals had visited on Walsh.

Jubal burst out laughing, "Well I'll be damned. I've got to hand it to you." He stopped laughing, his face and eyes turned hard, and he said, "Speakin' of hands." He pointed to Morgan's bandaged right hand. "I figure it was fifty, fifty between us, before. Now I think I can take you."

"Like I said, you think what you wanna think. But I think you've lived too long." Morgan thought, "His eyes will tell me. He's just 'bout talked himself into it."

"Farkle and Rideout were greenhorns." Jubal spread his legs and added, "Your ol' man was a coward." His hand moved like lighting, but his eyes had already betrayed his intentions.

Morgan's Colt shot six inches of flame and smoke just as Jubal's pistol started up. Morgan saw Jubal's eyes bulge in pain and surprise as the .45 slug slammed into his chest, the impact knocking him back two steps. Morgan stepped forward and fired again; the second bullet struck just to the left of the first, sending Jubal reeling backwards into the wall. As he slid down the wall, Morgan moved still closer and fired again. The third shot struck Jubal right between the eyes. Morgan watched stoically as Jubal sat down hard. After a brief moment, Jubal's lifeless body slumped to the right.

"Them first two were for my father." He holstered his pistol. "That last one is for Chris Walsh."

Chapter Twenty

Morgan stepped behind the bar and got a bottle and a glass, his thoughts running wild. "This one is different...I'm not thinking clear. I feel empty. Somethin's missin'. I always thought I'd feel good once I found him...killed him. Damn you, Jubal! You even cheated me out of th' satisfaction of seein' you dead."

He poured the whiskey as his mind began flashing back in time. Morgan saw his father, then the Kiowa brave, Devlin, Farkle, Leatherwood, Rideout, and Jubal. Then he saw just their faces as they died, one right after the other. Then he saw them all at the same time.

Morgan's hand began to tremble as he downed the drink.

When the burning liquid reached his stomach, all but one of the faces faded; the haunting eyes and face of the Kiowa brave remained. After a moment, it was joined by the face of Bear Paw.

Morgan poured another drink and whispered, "Bear Paw."

"What did you say?" asked Witherspoon.

Morgan looked up an saw Witherspoon and O'Banion. He saw Browne, who was standing over Jubal. Linda Farquar was standing just inside the door, staring at him with both shock and relief in her eyes. He hadn't seen any of them enter. "Careless of me," he said to himself. "Haven't done that before. Mistakes like that can get you killed."

Witherspoon spoke again. "Are you all right?"

Morgan was thinking clearly again. "Yeah…I'm all right. Did you get Piper locked up?"

"Tighter'n a drum," replied O'Banion. "He's madder'n a wet hen."

"Are you hurt?" asked Linda as she came up to them.

Morgan managed a faint smile. "I'm fine…just fine."

Browne whistled, "Crow's deader'n a doornail! Damn, Morgan. Why'd you kill a drunk? He ain't never hurt a fly."

Morgan smiled ruefully, "He ain't, huh?"

"Why hell no," sputtered Browne. "He maybe a—"

"Phil, shut up," interrupted O'Banion. He turned to Morgan and asked, "Where does Crow fit into all this?"

"First of all, his name isn't Joel Crow." Morgan poured himself another drink, downed it, and continued in a soft voice, "It's Jubal Carver. He killed my father."

Linda moved her hands to her mouth and gasped, "Killed your father?"

Morgan nodded his head. "And U. S. Marshall Chris Walsh."

"Walsh was a United States Marshall?" O'Banion scratched his chin. "I always knew there was something different about him. Why did they kill him?"

"I'm not sure. More'n likely he was on to 'em."

"I've got a newspaper to put out," Witherspoon said as he took out his pad and pencil. He looked questioningly at Morgan and added, "If you're up to it."

Morgan's mind was beginning to churn with all the things that still had to be done, but he said, "Sure. Why not?" He then briefed them on all that had occurred since he left Fort Worth. He finished by saying, "Myles, I'm a little bushed right now, and I've got me some thinkin' to do. How about I give you a detailed account tomorrow?"

Witherspoon put away his pad and pencil. "That's fine. I know you're—" The crack of the batwings slamming the wall made Witherspoon stop in mid-sentence.

Kyle Willson came storming in, all out of breath. "It's Piper! He just lit out, ridin' like a bat out of hell."

"Piper! How'd he…" Witherspoon turned to Morgan with a shocked look. He asked Willson. "Are you sure it was?"

"Hell yes, it was him. Myles, I can still see."

O'Banion held up the cell keys for all to see, and shrugged his shoulders. "I don't see how."

"It's my fault," Morgan quietly said. "He had another key. I should have searched him." Morgan asked Willson, "Was Burkett with Piper?"

"No, I don't think so. I didn't see him."

"Which way was he headed?"

Willson pointed south. "South. More'n likely for Mexico."

Morgan said to Browne, "Go check on Burkett."

"Sure thing, Marshall," Browne said as he hurried out.

By now the saloon had begun to fill up with townspeople. One of the men said, "I'll get some of th' boys. We'll form a posse and—"

Morgan interrupted and quietly said, "Thanks for th' offer, but it's my job. He'll keep 'til mornin'." He was thinking, "He knows I'll be comin' after him. I gotta feelin' he ain't gonna be goin' far."

Browne came back and announced, "Burkett's still locked up. Said he didn't kill anybody, didn't know nothin'."

Morgan smiled and started for the hotel. "Gotta get a wire off to McEachern and Dobby. They'll—" His thoughts were interrupted by Linda Farquar, who had caught up with him.

"Stuart, take some of the men. You can't do it alone. Your hand; it's—"

Morgan smiled at her, "No, they'd just be in th' way. There's been enough people hurt. Besides, like I said, it's my job." He held up his right hand. "It's feelin' better."

Linda knew by the look in his eyes and by the tone of his voice that it was useless to argue with him. "Can I help?"

"You can send a wire for me in th' mornin', if it's no bother."

"Oh, it's no bother," she said. "I'd be glad to."

"Thanks." Morgan walked away, but stopped suddenly and said, "When I get back, I was thinkin' about goin' for a buggy ride. I was wonderin' if you'd care to join me." He grinned and added, "That is, if you've made up your mind about me."

Linda laughed, "I have, and I will."

Morgan was on the move at daybreak. He picked up Piper's trail right off and thought, "I thought so. He's makin' no effort to hide his trail. A blind man could follow it. He wants me to catch up. Guess he's wantin' to end it, one way or th' other."

After an hour of following the signs and tracks, Morgan found where Piper stopped and waited. He studied the horse manure and cigarette papers that were left. "Nobody's that careless." He stroked Ebon's neck and mused, "Ebon, th' man's made up his mind. He's not gonna be taken alive." Morgan rode on and after a while and mused, "I made a promise to Chris Walsh. Piper's gettin' his…and that's a fact."

Morgan topped a sharp rise in the terrain and saw Piper just a hundred yards ahead; he was laying face up on the ground. His horse wasn't in sight. Morgan drew his Colt and thought, "Now what? Could be some kind of a trick, but I don't think so. Somethin' strange is goin' on. He looks dead." Morgan scanned the area and saw nothing to alarm him.

Morgan eased on down and stopped twenty yards or so from Piper's body. He holstered his pistol, stepped down, and said softly, "Bear Paw." Piper was naked, spread-eagled, and staked. Bear Paw's signature arrow was protruding from Piper's crotch; small fires around his hands, feet, and crotch area were still smoldering.

Morgan thought, "Damn! That's a hell of a way to die." Ebon suddenly snorted and skittered nervously away. Morgan spun around and drew his pistol with one motion.

Bear Paw sat his paint pony not fifty yards off. He gave the Plains hand sign for peace. Morgan put away his gun, made the sign for peace, and walked slowly toward Bear Paw, thinking, "He ain't wantin' to fight...wants to tell me somethin'. More'n likely why he killed Piper."

Bear Paw waited stoically until Morgan stopped in front of him, then he spoke quietly in Kiowa. "Hey, Morgan. I, Bear Paw." He pointed to Piper. "I give him to you."

Morgan answered in Kiowa. "I am grateful to Bear Paw. How does Bear Paw know my name? How does he know I speak the language of the People?"

Bear Paw touched his heart with his right fist. "Bear Paw knows many things. Morgan at Medicine Lodge. Spoke the language of the Kiowa, only white eyes who spoke the truth."

Morgan nodded his head, "Bear Paw has good memory. Perhaps he also remembers that day in the buffalo wallow when I killed a Kiowa warrior." Morgan knew he remembered, but he also knew that the Kiowas respected honesty and courage.

Bear Paw was silent for a long while before he said, "Bear Paw remembers like it was yesterday. My heart is still heavy. Two Feathers was my friend, my wife's brother."

"I wish there had been some other way. Like Bear Paw, my heart, too, is heavy."

"Morgan good man; not like other white eyes. They have no honor." He pointed once again to Piper. "They kill each other when they no see." He found Morgan's eyes and added. "There was no pleasure in your eyes that day."

"It is as you say. Bear Paw speaks the true truth." Morgan touched his heart. "But my heart is also heavy because of the road Bear Paw has taken."

Bear Paw looked all around as he held out his arms and replied, "All of this belonged to the Comanche and the Kiowa Nations. I don't want to travel the white man's road. I want to roam the prairies, hunt the buffalo. Even when the wolf is in my belly, I had rather eat dung and starve. This I said at Medicine Lodge. Bear Paw does not speak with the forked tongue." He gave the sign for speaks with a forked tongue.

Morgan nodded his head in agreement and asked, "What did this man do?"

Bear Paw showed emotion for the first time. He spat on the ground and said, "This one was marked by the Kiowa people. I, Bear Paw, swore an oath to all that the Kiowa hold sacred that he would not go unpunished."

Morgan nodded his head in agreement and waited for Bear Paw to continue.

Bear Paw held up his hand. "Five moons ago, that one sold the Kiowa stupid water. Three braves die…many sick. Turtle That Crawls." He ran his fingers across his eyes, "No see anymore."

Morgan and Bear Paw gazed into each other's eyes for several moments before Bear Paw jerked his paint pony around in a full circle and said, "Morgan, maybe we are brothers. Some time long ago, we suckled at the same mother. I must go now. We must not meet again in this world. These are my words." He made the sign for friend then rode slowly away, never looking back.

Morgan watched until Bear Paw disappeared over the horizon. He whistled for Ebon and said, "It's a damn shame. He's all alone...lost everything." Morgan climbed on Ebon and started slowly for Dog Bark.

After an hour of riding and thinking, Morgan whispered, "Ebon, I'm goin' for a buggy ride, no offense intended."

Ebon nickered quietly.